C000163084

The Imagination Gift

Dream One

The Kingdom of Chaos

MICAH J. KENNEY

Copyright © 2020 Micah J. Kenney.

All rights reserved. No part of this book may be used or reproduced by any means, graphic, electronic, or mechanical, including photocopying, recording, taping or by any information storage retrieval system without the written permission of the author except in the case of brief quotations embodied in critical articles and reviews.

LifeRich Publishing is a registered trademark of The Reader's Digest Association, Inc.

LifeRich Publishing books may be ordered through booksellers or by contacting:

LifeRich Publishing
1663 Liberty Drive
Bloomington, IN 47403
www.liferichpublishing.com
1 (888) 238-8637

Because of the dynamic nature of the Internet, any web addresses or links contained in this book may have changed since publication and may no longer be valid. The views expressed in this work are solely those of the author and do not necessarily reflect the views of the publisher, and the publisher hereby disclaims any responsibility for them.

Any people depicted in stock imagery provided by Getty Images are models, and such images are being used for illustrative purposes only. Certain stock imagery © Getty Images.

Scripture quotations marked KJV are from the Holy Bible, King James Version (Authorized Version). First published in 1611. Quoted from the KJV Classic Reference Bible, Copyright © 1983 by The Zondervan Corporation.

ISBN: 978-1-4897-2822-7 (sc)
ISBN: 978-1-4897-2821-0 (hc)
ISBN: 978-1-4897-2820-3 (e)

Library of Congress Control Number: 2020903804

Print information available on the last page.

LifeRich Publishing rev. date: 03/02/2020

Dedicated to God, Youngs Jersey Dairy,
My sister, Sarah, And the whole world

Contents

Chapter One
The Nothingness of Everything

This is a story about a young boy who had a gift, the imagination gift. Of course, everyone has the imagination gift, but very few learn how to use it to its maximum potential. Like anything in this life, to reach its maximum potential it must be founded in God. And that is the lesson that this young boy must learn as we all must. This young boy's name is Leonard Zacchaeus Whitten.

Leonard definitely lived up to his name. He was a wee little man, but yet, all nine-year-old boys are, since they haven't gone through puberty yet. He was scrawny and had shaggy, black hair that hung down to the top of his black, plastic-rimmed glasses. His bright, blue eyes seemed to hide behind the thickness of his lenses, but he didn't care. He was satisfied just to shake his long bangs out of his face, thinking it made him look *so* attractive. His young mind had been thwarted by his older friends that were fifteen-year-old, neighborhood boys, who had no boundaries set by their parents. Of course, Leonard's life wasn't much different…

The Whitten family lived in the RaMar Estates in Springfield, Ohio. Mr. David Whitten was married to his lovely wife, Jessica, and he was the proud owner of a rather successful family-owned investment company called, "Whitten & Company." They had three children. The eldest was an eighteen-year-old girl named Dana. She was as beautiful as her mother but used it in the wrong way. She had trouble staying with one guy for more than a month. Her sexually attractive attire didn't help her case much either. She was currently struggling to find the "perfect man" to be her date to senior prom at Shawnee High School. If only she knew what "perfect" actually was, she might just know what she was looking for.

David and Jessica Whitten also had a sixteen-year-old boy named Matthew, but he just went by Matt. He was handsome enough in his own little way, but he didn't seem to care very much. His eyes and brain had been corrupted by free internet access which was beginning to turn him toward drugs, as well. His "friend," Jack Stewart, at Shawnee didn't help either.

All this information seems quite depressing. They all got in the burgundy, Lexus RXL on Sunday to make a good appearance at Grace Mystery Church, which is a large church about fifteen minutes from where they live. Its pastor, John Kathlin, preaches powerful messages from the Word of Truth rightly divided, hence the Church name's focus on the Grace Message of Ephesians 2:8-9, "For by grace are ye saved through faith; it is the gift of God: Not of works, lest any man should boast."

Even though the Whittens had the Truth preached to them every Sunday, they failed to apply it to their lives. God was about to give them all a wakeup call by using, wouldn't you guess, a dream. From the outside, the Whittens look like they have everything, but not to their backdoor neighbors, Joseph and Arlene Dubacht.

Joseph and Arlene Dubacht were an elderly German couple that were obviously German Baptist, as you could tell from his long, bushy gray beard that lacked a mustache and her silver hair tied up with a bonnet to cover it all. Joseph and Arlene snuffed their noses at the Whittens' wealth even though they were living in the same area, the RaMar *Estates*. They were definitely some strange folk. To the self-righteous Dubachts, the Whittens had "Nothing whatsoever of eternal wealth." And they weren't afraid to tell them that either.

Well, David Whitten's family-owned investment company might have been successful, but neither one of his elder kids wanted any part in it. They both told him, "I want to strike out on my own and make a difference." Their father's response somewhat surprised them. "Well, you're still going to have to work *somewhere*." And so, their "difference making" just happened to start at the Golden Jersey Inn of Young's Jersey Dairy in Yellow Springs. Dana worked as a waitress there, while Matt was just a busser boy.

One Friday, at the rather large office building in Dayton, Ohio, David Whitten walked into the wide-open office space from lunch and his young and beautiful secretary, Cyndi Dunne, was rather anxious to bring her work files to him from her desk that sat just outside his office. The office space was set up with three curved, white, blocky desks in the main area and then David's room at the end with his desk.

Cyndi was wearing a rather alluring outfit that would definitely catch one's eye, but that's not what David noticed. He just politely received the paperwork and said, "Your perfume smells nice today, Miss Dunne."

She just playfully batted her mascara-accented, hazel eyes and smoothed her auburn hair as she sweetly replied, "Thank you, Mr. Whitten."

"Mr. Whitten" quickly popped out the doorway to his office and said, "How many times do I have to tell you to call me David. We're all friends here." He smiled back at her and that wasn't the best thing he could've done just then. She took it a bit differently than he meant it and sort of swaggered back to her desk, giving him "the eye."

David didn't notice it because he just ducked back into his office, but another one of his employees did. She was a thin, Christian, black woman named Demira Jacksan. She just stood next to Nathan Carter's desk, where she had just placed some receipts, because that was her job. She kept track of the receipts, while Nathan Carter kept track of the public…and her. You see, this tall, thin, black, college basketball player had a thing for Miss Demira Jackson and just stared at her as she stood by his desk with her left hand on her hip. He also liked that her desk was right across from his, so whenever he looked up, there she was.

She was wearing a white and black work skirt and shirt, but it was far more decent than Cyndi's. She also had her long, straight, black hair done up in a bun atop her head.

"Well, I'll be, if she ain't playin' her Eve to his Adam. Just rubbin' that forbidden fruit right under his nose, so he can sure *smell* it," whispered Demira, unknowingly in Nathan's hearing.

Nathan leaned toward her in his desk chair as his semi-muscular arms flexed from the exertion of pushing his body forward, "What do you mean?" His light purple, dress shirt also became tight on his pecs as his dark purple tie just hung forward with his body. He was a fan of purple; in case you couldn't tell.

Demira cocked her head toward him with her beautiful brown eyes opened wide and began waving her finger around, "I'm talkin' about how she's got her googly eyeballs going *all* over him." She moved her finger in a circular motion when she spoke about how much of David's body Cyndi was looking at.

"I'm still not gettin' it," stated Nathan as he looked toward David's office and shook his head in confusion. He was a Christian and went to church, too, but sometimes he was just dense.

Demira just continued to gape at Nathan's denseness and then nodded her head toward David's office, "You mean you don't see that?"

"See what?"

Demira just smirked and added, "Never mind. I just remembered who I was askin'."

Nathan leaned back in his chair in shock, "What's that supposed to mean?"

Demira had started walking back to her own desk, but quickly turned around, "It means men are *blind.*"

Nathan just smiled and used this opportunity for some flirtin', "Unless I only got eyes for you." He winked after he spoke.

Demira smiled and playfully reached her hand toward his desk, "Aw, honey..." Her face quickly went deadpan, "No." She briskly walked back to her desk and began straightening it up as she muttered to herself, "I don't see why Mr. Whitten's taken the time to smell *Cyndi's* perfume, when he's got a beautiful wife waitin' for him at home?"

"What're you sayin' over there?" asked Nathan as he leaned back in his chair with his left leg resting on top of his right.

Demira just continued to look down and shake her head as she worked, "Doesn't matter, 'cause I wasn't talkin' to you."

"Well, how was I supposed to know that?" asked Nathan as he flipped around the pencil in his right hand.

Demira finally looked up at him with a slight glare, "Because if I was talkin' to you, I would have yelled it, because I know you're *deaf.*"

Nathan just smiled in his amusement, again, "Man, I just got all kinds of problems. First, I'm blind and then I'm deaf. Next you'll be tellin' me I can't even talk."

Demira struggled not to smile, too, as she finally sat down in her chair and swiveled toward her computer. She glanced back, but then just shook her head.

Meanwhile, on the way home from work...

Matt tried to be a "good" older brother to Leonard, but that didn't get him farther than encouraging his wild imagination. Matt knew Leonard was obsessed with Chinese mythology and had thought up a joke to encourage him.

Matt had just arrived home to his large, white house that sat in the middle of the RaMar Estates, after working a day shift, because yesterday had been his final day of school for the semester. He drove his own silver Lexus RC up the U-shaped, asphalted driveway and parked on the square concrete section that was in front of the large, two-car garage. In case you couldn't tell, the Whittens went big on *everything.* Strange how appearances can be misleading.

Matt stepped up and out of his low-riding car with his "super star" black sunglasses on his face. It was almost summer, so the weather was heating up and getting ready for all that sunbathing. Matt's skin was just slightly tanned, but that didn't stop him from rocking the "super star" look with his blonde hair in a Fauxhawk. He also had a decent amount of muscle, as you could tell from his bicep flexing to close his car door. He tried to accent his figure even more by buying T-shirts that were too small for him. He also generally wore some sort of shorts that would show off his lower leg muscles. He even wore them in the winter time. But today, he was just wearing his red and black, work uniform. The girls tended to smile and wave when he came around pushing that bussing cart with his "oh-so-muscular" arms. He tended to just give them a "what's up" and then move on.

Of course, today, he was in a better mood, so he did a little bit more than just nod his head upward. He smiled, too, because he was pleased with himself and excited to tell Leonard his little joke. He opened the front door and swaggered in with his typical "I'm so awesome" attitude. He stood in the long, tile floor entryway, standing on the rectangle, gray rug that served to decorate the floor and wipe off the dirt on your shoes.

Matt was young and rebellious, so he didn't wipe off his shoes or take them off. He just quickly ran up the stairs that were at the end of the long entryway and dirtied up the soft, ivory carpet that was all over the house. White banisters went up each side of the stairs that he used to launch himself up multiple steps at a time, hoping his mom wouldn't hear him, but she did. She quickly came running around from the kitchen that was to the left of the staircase and yelled up the stairs, "Matthew David Whitten, you take your shoes off right now!" Her flowing, long, black hair swayed forward from her momentum of turning the corner. She brushed it back behind her ear as she walked away and heard Matt cackle sinisterly. He thought getting in trouble was amusing.

Jessica just dried her hands on the dish cloth in her hands and shook her head. She had bright brown eyes that gleamed through her mascara as she struggled not to smile. She had had a good day, too. Her trip to the salon and spa had gone very well. She was quite pleased with the *beautiful* results and couldn't wait to see if her husband would notice…this time. She tried very hard to please him, but he didn't seem to gaze her way much anymore with his bright baby blues. He might have been bald at a young age with just the blonde hair in his eyebrows left on his face, but his blue eyes could still make a girl smile. He was rather muscular built, too. That's why he encouraged Matt's weight training. Matt and he got along quite well, because Matt was kind of the spittin' image of him. After all, Matt had baby blue eyes, too.

In fact, David was the next one to walk through the front door, wearing his signature, light gray suit and blue tie that accented his eyes. Jessica heard him come in and quickly turned on her heels and tossed the dish cloth through the doorway to the kitchen and onto the stainless-steel island in the middle. She quickly tried to pull her outfit a little tighter on her hips and press out her figure. It wasn't hard, because her dressy outfit was already pretty tight on her figure and probably something someone her age shouldn't be wearing. But it was all in the "good cause" to please her husband.

As he turned the corner, she had just finished touching up her hair from the quick turn to scorn Matt. David walked up to his wife and the first thing he said was a question, "Why'd you get your hair done?" He innocently unbuttoned his suit coat and loosened his tie with his right hand, because his left one was occupied with holding his briefcase.

Jessica would've gone to tears if David hadn't just walked around her, after her delayed time to respond, and asked another question, "So what's for dinner?"

She barely kept it in as she continued to stare toward the front door and gently answer, "Beef pot roast with baked potatoes." It was something easy for her to make while she was at the salon and spa, because you just have to put it in a crock pot for a couple of hours. She continued, struggling to stay calm, "It'll be ready in an hour." She finally decided to brave his gaze and turned toward him.

He just looked at her, gave a fake-sort-of smile, and stated, "Good. I'm going to go soak in the tub." With that said, he just walked right on up the stairs. You see, all the bedrooms were upstairs to allow ample amount of room downstairs for "things." Things like a living room, TV room, kitchen, half-bath for guests, and the dining room with an exquisite view of their pool through the French doors. The basement was basically a big rec room with the whole nine yards: a pool table, ping pong table, air hockey table, *and* a foosball table. There also was a large, flat screen TV for "video-gaming."

After David went up, Dana came running down in her work uniform, because she had a night shift. Without saying a word to her mother, she leapt out the front door. She and her mother seemed to be on a "need to talk" basis, even though they looked a lot alike. Dana had dreamy brown eyes, too, which made her a triple threat with great hair, great eyes, and great body; also, her tanned and smooth skin.

Meanwhile, Matt burst into Leonard's room that was on the end of the hallway and had a decent view of the pool. His room was up the stairs and to the left in the hallway that ran horizontally in the upstairs.

Leonard perked up from playing with his Lego figures and gazed through his thick lenses at his intruding brother. After all, he was in the middle of an epic battle. Matt just smiled at the way his nerdy brother tried to glare at him.

Eventually, Leonard spoke up in a dry tone, "I'm assuming you have collateral for the damage you have caused?"

Matt smirked and then knelt down beside his little brother on the floor. "I sure do, buddy. I've got a story idea I think you might be interested in..." You see, Leonard loved to make up full-fledged stories with his Lego figures. That's just how strong his imagination was for his age. Most of the stories had to do with Chinese mythology, so that's why Matt was so excited to tell him his idea.

Leonard just looked up and over his glasses and said, "Keep talkin'."

"Well, hear it is, pal...So it's about a kingdom where no ruler remains on the throne for an entire day, because they're constantly in battle. The kingdom's name is Bu Zing." Matt somewhat smiled and kept nodding his head, greatly anticipating what Leonard's response would be.

Leonard just started looking through his thick lenses at his older brother, again, "Why so specific on the name of the kingdom?"

Matt somewhat smirked in surprise of his little brother's smartness, but then proceeded to explain, "Well, you see, I was working in *bussing* at work today and it's kind of like the kingdom."

"So, you made it sound Chinese by calling it, 'Bu Zing'?" Leonard began nodding his head to show that he approved, "Clever."

With that said, Matt roughed up Leonard's shaggy hair and added, "See ya later, buddy. I got stuff to do." After he walked out of Leonard's room, he stopped in the hallway to listen. He was happy to hear Leonard start working with his story idea. He smiled and then walked down the hallway to his room. His room was down the hallway that ran horizontally in front of the stairs and then to the right at the end of another hallway that ran perpendicular to the one he was in. So basically, it was just one big, L-shaped hallway.

Once you walked in, you could definitely tell it was a teenage boy's room. Some might say it's just the typical way for a teenage boy's room to look, but I don't think pictures of indecent women splashed all over the walls should be the "typical" appearance of a teenage boy's room. Well, at least you know now why there's a "Keep out!" sign on his door. The strange thing is that his parents actually obey it, as if their son is the one with the authority that God gave them as his parents. But yet, I guess the Word of God means nothing to those who would rather hear the soothsaying of a psychologist telling them, "Rebelling at their age is just the norm. It can even be 'healthy'. You should just let them be themselves."

The thing is, if you let people "be themselves," "themselves" in their natural forms are sinners. But with God, their identity of "themselves" is worth living out, because it has changed from the old man and become the new. So, says 2 Corinthians 5:17.

As you can see, from the outside, everything seemed fine and awesome with the Whittens, but when it came to reality, they were falling apart at the seams. They had *everything*, but it amounted to *nothing*. That night, the whole family could hear the seams ripping in the master bedroom as their parents quarreled over what each other deserved.

Chapter Two
Confrontation without Correction

The next morning, everyone wanted to get away from home. Running from what needs to be confronted seemed the most logical response to them. David and Matt went to the gym then Matt was going to go to his "friend's" house. Dana and Leonard conspired to have their friends over, while Jessica just got up and started the chores…alone. Something seems wrong with this picture.

After David and Matt left, Leonard and Dana came running down the stairs at the same time. They waltzed through the sitting room and into the kitchen where their mom stood, putting the breakfast dishes in the dishwasher. She stood by the small window above the dishwasher's counter as the morning sun shone through and cast its rays upon her. She looked quite picturesque, but neither one of her kids noticed that about their mom. They just wanted to get their "communication" over with.

As soon as Jessica turned toward them, they both said at the same time, "I'm having some friends over." They looked at each other, surprised, and then just turned back to their mom.

Jessica's first instinct after barely getting a night's sleep was to scorn them for not asking her first, but then she heard that psychologist's voice in the back of her head saying, "Don't aggravate them. They're in a delicate stage of their lives. You just need to let them be." A pity that it was a psychologist's voice nagging in the back of her mind and not the Word of God. Otherwise, she would have taken her God-given authority over her children, but all she thought to do was smooth her bangs back toward the ponytail the rest of her hair was in and sigh. When she looked up, she breathed in her tired voice, "That's fine. I just wish you would've asked me first."

Dana's quick response was typical for her age, but that didn't make it right, "Why? I'm eighteen, Mom. I can make my own decisions without input."

Leonard just stared at his older sister in surprise and then sheepishly pointed at her with eyes fixed on his mom, "Yeah, what she said."

Jessica just looked down at her baby boy and dryly said, "You're nine."

There was a strong pause and then Leonard started clapping his hands slowly together, "Soooooo?"

Jessica, once again, sighed in defeat, "Fine, are they staying for dinner?"

Dana was the first to answer as she pulled out her Smartphone, "No, we'll probably just go out for pizza."

Jessica looked down at Leonard and he gave his typical shrug as if to say, "I don't know."

Jessica just nodded her head, a bit annoyed, and cattily stated, "I'll just plan on two more for dinner. Now just go on." She waved her hand at them to leave.

Dana and Leonard walked out of the kitchen feeling like livestock that had just been herded. It was awkward, but Dana just shook it off and began texting her "girlfriends" to bring their swimsuits. Leonard dwelt on the awkwardness a little bit longer than she did, but then he saw what she was texting and became overjoyed. He ran upstairs to his room and began texting Kyle and Caleb to come over quick, because Dana and her friends were going to go swimming.

After he finished sending his texts, he sat back against his headboard on his bed and began to use his imagination for the wrong things. He began to imagine those "Baja beauties" around the pool. If only Dana knew what she was doing to her brother by promoting immodesty to him as attractive. Really, everyone was. Mostly Kyle and Caleb, though. They're the fifteen-year-old boys that had input "mature" thoughts into Leonard's mind, but they didn't care. They didn't go to church and they most certainly *weren't* Christians.

David arrived back home that afternoon, but only to tell his wife, "Sorry, but I just found out I need to go into work today. Cyndi and I have some work to finish." He didn't even wait for a response from Jessica. He just galloped upstairs to "freshen up" before putting on his suit and tie to go to "work."

His exit was as quick as his entrance. He left without giving his wife even the slightest show of affection. Tears began to form in her eyes as she felt doubts pounding on her brain. The echo was almost more than she could bear as she walked back into the kitchen to get the sweeper out of the closet that was in between the doorways of the sitting room and kitchen. She was gonna try and work it off in her chore clothes, which were a button-down, faded, denim shirt and gray leggings.

About half an hour later, while she was sweeping the entryway rug, Matt peeked his head through the front door and she was quite shocked, in her present state, at what she saw. Matt's face was somewhat pale and his eyes were bloodshot with eyelids flying at half-mast. He tried to act like they didn't make eye contact as he scooted around her and the sweeper.

Jessica began to hear new doubts pounding, but these were about her son's health. They were just fed by the fact that he was trying to sneak past her. She began to try and think of what the proper approach would be from a psychological perspective. Eventually, when he was halfway up the stairs, she asked, "What'd you guys do at your friend's house?"

He turned around and almost fell down the stairs from the sudden movement, but he caught himself on the banisters. He wasn't using them to spring himself up the stairs today. "Oh, we just played a lot of videogames, so I'm gonna go rest in my room." He thought that was a convincing enough lie to sway the vote.

Jessica just nodded her head and gave a fake smile, "Okay." She was just getting hit from left and right today and she felt like the only one responsible. That's a lot for her to bear as a mom.

Once she finished the entryway, everybody started bursting through the front door to dirty up the rug she'd just swept off. First, were Kyle and Caleb. They didn't even say "hello" to Jessica, who was standing off to the right side of the stairs in the living room. They just ran right upstairs, hoping they hadn't missed a thing.

Next, all the girls funneled in with pool bags draping from their shoulders. All of them were just friends from school, except for one. She was a friend from church and definitely Christian, as you could tell from her actually noticing the poor, tired woman standing right next to her. "Hello, Mrs. Whitten. How are you?" She extended her hand.

That brightened up Jessica's weary face as she shook the girl's hand, "Oh, I'm just fine, Jennifer." The girl's full name was Jennifer Thompson.

The Thompsons were some very nice people that just wanted to help everybody. Britt and Theresa Thompson were the most happily married couple you ever did see with a beautiful seventeen-year-old daughter and bright five-year-old little girl. They had no boys, so Britt felt the need to raise his daughters to be strong.

Eventually, all the girls were around the pool in their swimsuits as Leonard and his friends spied on them from his "perfect view" window. Every last one of them was wearing some sort of bikini, except, wouldn't you guess, Jennifer Thompson. She was wearing a nice one-piece that was modest and accented her eyes. Leonard couldn't help but feel a little uneasy about them gaping at his sister with his own binoculars, because that's where Kyle and Caleb's stare was mainly aimed. They *both* had the hots for his sister, even though they were *only* fifteen.

When Leonard was finally given a turn on the binoculars, he began to think, "Jennifer looks the prettiest, but how can that be? She's just wearing a one-piece. That's not attractive, or is it?" It's truthful that 'the spirit is willing, but the flesh is weak,' because Leonard quickly forced himself to fix his gaze upon the other girls.

When it was time for Kyle or Caleb to take a turn, they both grabbed the binoculars at the same time. They went into a death glare, and then Kyle piped up, "I want them to look at my future girlfriend."

"Oh, yeah? Well, so do I!" responded Caleb as he pulled the binoculars toward himself.

Kyle yanked them back and practically snarled, "Oh, yeah? Well, who's that?!" Their voices had begun to rise and Leonard was afraid his mom might hear them.

"Dana!" answered Caleb as he yanked the binoculars back toward himself and Kyle, surprisingly, let go. Caleb was, at first, pleased, but then realized his exertion from pulling on the binoculars had now made him off balance. When he looked up, he saw an angry Kyle coming at him with fists raised saying, "She's mine."

Suddenly, the two boys began to brawl, while Leonard tried to stop them, but he was just a "wee little man," so what could he do?

Jessica was still sweeping and the vacuum was loud enough that she couldn't hear the ruckus.

While Kyle and Caleb brawled it out with the door closed, Dana came into the house, wrapped in a colorful beach towel to try and keep from getting the carpet wet. She came in to ask Matt to come out, because some of the girls wanted to see him. As she ascended the steps, she heard commotion coming from behind Leonard's closed door, but didn't think anything of it.

"They're probably just playing a videogame," thought Dana to herself, after all, Leonard did have a flat screen TV and Xbox One in his bedroom.

She just continued on down the hallway toward the turn that led toward Matt's bedroom. She didn't pay attention to the sign on the door and just burst in to a regretful experience. She saw her own brother gaping at something on his computer screen that made her, as his sister, very embarrassed to know he was looking at it.

Matt quickly clicked the "X" at the top right corner of his computer screen and leapt up from his desk chair to stand in front of her, "What? I'm busy."

Dana just crossed her arms, cocked her hips to one side, and raised her left eyebrow, "Oh, busy lookin' at that garbage?" She suddenly noticed his eyes, "And probably poppin' a few at Jack's house?" She began to stand up straight as Matt just stood there and took her punches, "Do you know what Mom and Dad would do if they knew?"

Matt finally burst in his defense, "What'd you care?! You're dressed the same way under that towel and you lie around the pool for everybody to see!"

Dana just rolled her eyes, but felt a little offended, "You're hopeless, Matt."

Matt began to glare at his sister, "No! This *family* is hopeless!" He quickly slammed his door in her face so hard that the frame moved.

They didn't know it, but Jessica had heard them, because she was right under where they were and had come to the steps. She heard every word and tears began to burn in her eyes. She then heard Dana coming toward the stairs and quickly tried to hide beside them.

Dana walked right down the steps and turned right to go through the sitting room and kitchen to get to the dining room, which is where the exit to the pool was. Dana didn't see her mom, shaking with tears, crouched by the stairs on the living room side.

As Dana walked, she ripped off her beach towel and sought to flaunt herself in her black bikini. Due to the pace at which she walked and her loose apparel, it made her walk rather undignified. The more and more she tried to convince herself she wasn't doing anything wrong, the more she began to feel disturbed that her own brother had just compared her to porn. She seemed distant to her friends for the rest of the day.

Suddenly, inside, Jessica heard another loud voice come from Leonard's room saying, "I never want to see you again!"

Kyle and Caleb came running down the steps with bumps and bruises from their fighting and quickly exited. Jessica became curious as she heard Leonard begin to cry a little, too. Leonard had grown tired of his "used-to-be" friends and he was really ticked off when they broke his binoculars in their bickering. For some reason, he also seemed upset with them for lusting after his sister, but he didn't understand why. It felt like something was working inside of him and he didn't know what or Who it was. The whole situation just caused him to cry as he slowly, thoughtfully shut his door.

Jessica just sat there, not realizing the home phone in the kitchen was ringing. Eventually, it went to voicemail and she heard the voice of her husband leaving a message, "Hey, its David. I just wanted to let you know that you don't have to set a place for me at the table. Cyndi and I have to work late. Ummmm, bye!"

Jessica couldn't take it anymore. She didn't know what she was doing wrong as thoughts of betrayal just flooded her brainwaves. The one person she thought to turn to was her backdoor neighbor, Arlene Dubacht. That wasn't the best decision and she probably would have realized that if she had been in her right mind. She just quickly stood up and speed-walked out the back of the house through the garage. She didn't want the girls to see her balling her eyes out.

Finally, she reached the Dubacht's front door and tried to collect herself. She smoothed out her hair and tried to wipe the tears off her cheeks before knocking on the large, wooden door with glass windows and a gold knob. The Dubacht's house was large like the Whitten's, but its color scheme was different. It had a primary color of tan and a secondary color of burgundy.

Arlene Dubacht's bonneted head became visible through the windows as the expression on her face almost told Jessica what she was whispering under her breath, "Lord Almighty, drunken Hannah's on my front porch?!"

"Drunken Hannah" saw Arlene's countenance quickly change to a big, white smile as she opened the door and asked, "Vhat be troublin' you, Mrs. Vhitten?" She tried to press out her aqua green and white-checkered, cape dress as she looked at Jessica through her circular, silver-rimmed glasses, waiting for an answer. It took a little while before she remembered her manners. They finally came to her after a brief moment of staring into Jessica's tearful eyes. She quickly added, "Oh, dearie, vhy don't zou come in and ve can discuss it over a nice cup of tea?"

Jessica finally gathered the courage enough to say something as she sniffed, "Thank you, Mrs. Dubacht. I'm sorry for the sudden intrusion. I just didn't know who else to talk to."

Arlene helped Jessica in and then closed the fancy door behind her, "Don't vory, Mrs. Vhitten. Ya not be intrudin'. Joseph is just in zere vatchin' his football." Like I said, they were some strange folk, "OSU's playin', odhervise it vouldn't be on zat channel." There was a brief pause and then she added, "It'd be on Hallmark." Their only child, Abram, had graduated from OSU. That's why they liked to watch their games, and they were just plain, downright Ohioans.

Jessica couldn't help but laugh a little through her tears as Arlene pointed her toward the kitchen that was just down the stained, wooden floor hallway. Those floors ran all over their house. Arlene took a step toward the living room where her husband was watching his football and yelled, "Joseph?!"

"Ya?" responded Joseph as he continued to sit on the brown and black plaid couch and watch the scarlet and gray beat the pants off their opponents.

Arlene leaned toward the doorway as she continued to shout at her husband, "I'll just be in ze kitchen, havin' tea with Mrs. Vhitten!"

"Alright," was Joseph's simple and direct answer. He had become accustomed to listening to his wife tell him every little detail that happened in the world and had learned to deal with it by short responses to try and hurry his wife to the end.

Arlene squeaked her way down the hallway toward the kitchen, because she was a little on the hefty side. When she arrived, she found Jessica already sitting down at the small, circular, wooden table in the corner across from the doorway. Most everything in the Dubacht's house was made of stained wood and accented with a lit candle in almost every room. You could also find many quilts about and knitted and crocheted objects. Mrs. Dubacht liked to work with her hands and her mouth. Those were her two most valuable tools...to her.

She walked over to the stove and poured them some hot tea. She handed Jessica a cup and then sat down across from her, while stirring it with a metal spoon. Jessica just stared at her own cup as she did the same. She seemed to have calmed down a little. Finally, Arlene looked up over her glasses and asked, "So vhat be troublin' ya, Jessica?"

Jessica looked up from her cup as her lip quivered and she tried to withhold her tears, "Everything."

Arlene raised both her eyebrows as she placed her spoon on the table, gripped the handle to her cup, and sighed with eyes fixed downward, "Vell, zat not be very informative."

Jessica suddenly realized who she was talking to and struggled to keep in the frustration as you could hear her spoon start clinking the cup harder. Eventually, she looked up and stated, "My family is falling apart and I don't know what to do about it."

Arlene placed her cup back on the table after taking a sip and leaned back in her chair with somewhat of a smile, "Vell now, zat *is* explicit." She leaned back forward and Jessica suddenly felt the need to ventilate, "The thing is, Dana's getting more and more distant, actually, they all are. David doesn't even say 'hello' anymore or show me any affection. Matt keeps himself locked away in his room doing who knows what and is probably doing drugs." Arlene's eyes got so big they looked like they were gonna pop out of her head or her lenses were gonna shatter, but Jessica didn't notice. She just kept right on venting, "I left Leonard at home crying alone for an unknown reason, and on top of all that, my husband…" She began to cry, "My husband is working late with his young and *beautiful* secretary and he could be cheating on me for all I know."

There was a long pause as Jessica tried to calm herself back down, while Arlene just gave her a blank stare. Arlene simply stood up, walked over to the counter, and brought a box of tissues to the table. She sat down heavily in her chair as it sounded like it was going to give way to her plop and then she cupped her hands in her lap. She just sat there and watched as Jessica made use of tissue after tissue.

Finally, Arlene's blank stare broke and she simply said, "Perhaps, yer lookin' to ze wrong vone to help you?"

Jessica sniffed and tried to answer, "If you're talking about God, I don't know why He hasn't helped already?"

Arlene leaned in close and let her self-righteous advice rain down, "Zat's because you haven't given God a reason to be helpin', Jessica. Are you really tryin' to please Him? Because it be soundin' like yer just not good enough fer Him to be ahelpin' you…"

That last sentence echoed in Jessica's mind as everything else went silent around her and she just stared, trying to keep tears from flowing. The truth is, she was too petrified to cry. Everything seemed to be going wrong. All the walls were crashing down on her and she was too weak to try and hold them up. She felt so crushed that she didn't even notice Arlene ushering her out the front door and saying, "Goodbye, Mrs. Vhitten. I'm sorry about yer problem, but it be appearin' that yer on yer own."

The sun had hidden behind some clouds now and a chilling breeze blew against her as she strolled back to her house. The weather had begun to mirror her mood. She had her arms wrapped around herself, trying to comfort herself and keep herself warm. Her legs began to feel cold, too, since she was just wearing leggings. It just made her feel worse as she eventually walked into her own kitchen. As she glanced out the French doors in the dining room, she noticed that the girls were all gone now and the pool was still, just like her heart. Blue and still.

Eventually, Leonard came down the stairs because he was hungry. Matt didn't come because he was passed out on his bed. A side effect from the drugs he took. Leonard was moping around, too, and found his mom curled up in a ball on their big, brown, leather couch in the sitting room. He struggled to speak to her as she just blankly stared at the daisies in the vase on the marble coffee table in the center of the room, "Um, I'm hungry." He didn't think to actually ask what was for dinner.

Through all this chaos, Jessica had forgotten to make dinner. It just made her feel worse, but she tried to do her best for her son. She looked toward him with glistening tears in her eyes, "Um, how about we just make up some pizza rolls? Do you know if Matt's hungry?"

Leonard appeared to look around in confusion, "Um, no. I don't think he is."

Jessica tried to smile as she stood up and walked toward the kitchen, "Alright, then let's get them out of the freezer."

They ate, just the two of them, at the table that night. Jessica didn't even bless the food, because she doubted if God would actually hear her. After all, she wasn't good enough for Him to spend His time with her, was she? At least that's the way she was thinking now, if you can call it that.

They just stared at their plates and didn't say a word to each other. They *both* had a lot on their mind. Leonard sat in a chair that caused his gaze to be toward the pool. All he could see was visions of the girls lying around it from earlier. The thoughts plagued his mind as sorrow cast itself over the entire Whitten household.

Meanwhile, at the office building in Dayton, Ohio, David and Cyndi were working late after ordering-in Chinese food. They were in David's office at his desk. He sat in his chair as she sat across from him, making googly eyes at him the whole night. Finally, she decided to make an advancement toward him. As she handed him a file and he took it in his hand, she let her hand ever-so-slightly slide onto his. She gave it a slight caress, but she underestimated David's response. He quickly withdrew his hand as the file slapped onto the desktop.

Suddenly, as he looked across his desk at his secretary smiling with her left eyebrow raised, he felt a great pain in his gut. It was a churning feeling that felt like he had been run-through by a javelin. He tried as politely as possible to stand up and say, "Um, will you excuse me?"

Cyndi just continued to smile as she flipped her hair back and simply said, "Of course."

David just as quickly as possible made his way to the restroom. He found himself leaning on the sink counter in front of the mirrors just staring at his reflection. He eventually splashed some water on his face, trying to awaken himself from the tempted daze he was in, as if he could wash it all away. He continued to feel that churning within him and suddenly found himself seeking Heavenly help, "Lord, what am I doing? I shouldn't be here with her alone. What should I do?" He looked over at the door as it seemed to taunt him.

Suddenly, a feeling of boldness came over him and he flung the restroom door open. He walked back into his office where Cyndi was anxiously waiting. His glance in her direction was very quick as he cleared his throat and closed the open files on his desk. He looked up and simply stated, "It's late, Cyndi. We should just go home."

"But all the work isn't done."

"We still should just leave." David tried to seem firm, but the truth was, his knees were about ready to buckle under the pressure of her eyes.

Cyndi took this chance for another advancement toward David, "To my place?"

It took David longer to answer than it should have, but he did the right thing in the end, "No. You need to go home to *your* place, and I need to go home to *my* home, where *my wife* is waiting for me."

Cyndi just stood up and tried to maintain her dignity after her failed attempt, "Fine. Settle for less if you want to, but you could have had more." She flung her purse over her shoulder and swaggered out of his office.

When the office door closed behind her, David sighed heavily and fell upon his desk with his hands. That had taken the wind right out of him, but he still had his dignity intact, unlike Cyndi. He just stood there for a little while, catching his breath and gathering his thoughts back together. He eventually took a seat in his desk chair as he rubbed his chin and continued to ponder the night's experience.

After the girls left the pizza parlor, Dana swiped her credit card to pay for the meal at the checkout counter and Jennifer waited at the door for some reason.

Dana put her credit card in her purse and then walked to the front door where she was surprised to see Jennifer waiting on her. She resituated her purse strap so it was on the strap to her black tank top and asked, "Why are you still here?"

Jennifer just looked at Dana with gentle, blue eyes that went with her wavy, blonde hair and touched her hand to Dana's arm, "Are you okay, Dana? You haven't seemed yourself lately."

Dana felt like a burden just fell on her shoulders as tears began to swell in her eyes from the kindness of her *true* friend. She adjusted her purse strap, again, as she tried to refrain from letting the tears fall down her face, but a few slipped out. She glanced down in defeat and then back up to Jennifer's eye level as she bit her lip, but then simply stated, "I think my family's falling apart."

At first, Jennifer didn't know what to say, but then she leaned toward Dana still with her gentle gaze, "Do you feel like talking about it?"

Dana just smirked with a sniff as she walked past Jennifer, "No, thanks." She walked out the door as Jennifer replied, "I'll be praying for you!"

Jennifer just stood there, feeling like she had just taken on some of Dana's burden.

That night, at the Thompson's small house, they gathered in their living room for their prayer time before going to bed. They did this every night and tonight it was Jennifer's turn to start. She started their family prayer that night, praying for the Whittens.

Chapter Three

Warfare

On Sunday morning, no one really talked to each other at the Whitten's house, because they all got up at different times. It was usually later than they should, but still they continued to sleep in. Jessica was the first one up, then Leonard, then Dana, then Matt, and then finally, David. They all bustled about trying to eat breakfast and get ready for church at the same time. They generally went to Sunday school *and* the morning service, just trying to maintain a good image.

Whenever someone's eyes would meet, they'd quickly look away from each other or find something else to occupy their gaze. Leonard noticed this because he was the only one actually sitting at the table eating his bowl of cereal. Everyone else was just grabbing a slice of toast or making pop tarts. Not really a sufficient breakfast, but they were in a hurry.

This Sunday morning, Dana felt a little hesitant to wear her skin tight, short-skirted, green dress that she normally did, but then gave in. She couldn't stop thinking about what Matt had said the day before and that's what caused her to hesitate.

Matt cared about how he looked this morning, trying to hide the lasting effects of the drugs he took yesterday. He greased his hair, put on deodorant and cologne, and made sure to wear clothes that didn't clash, which was a navy blue, short-sleeve polo with tan, cargo shorts. His look was completed with his brown flip-flops.

Leonard was just a typical nine-year-old boy who didn't really care what he wore. He just threw some clothes on that would fit and slipped on his geeky sneakers.

David just dressed up like he was going to work, while his wife took forever trying to look perfect. She was fighting a battle that no human could win on their own: the fight for perfection.

Eventually, they all climbed into their Lexus RXL with David in the driver's seat, Jessica riding shotgun as she tried to put on the last layers of her makeup, Dana - behind her mom, Matt - behind his dad, and Leonard - just in the back. Once everyone had on their seatbelts, David pulled out of the now open garage and down the driveway to the street.

The fifteen-minute drive to Grace Mystery Church seemed especially long this morning, because no one wanted to say anything. Jessica didn't even turn on Air1 like she normally did on Sundays. *Only* on Sundays, in fact. She wasn't "feelin' it" today and she knew the kids didn't really like that kind of music, anyway. They preferred the "rap trash" circulated around school.

All the kids just had their phones out and ear buds in, so David began to wonder if he should take this time to tell Jessica about last night's victory over temptation or not. His thoughts were something like this, "I betcha she'd be proud, although, she'd probably just say we shouldn't have been alone together in the first place and not give me the pat on the back I deserve…" He just decided not to say anything, after his "reasoning." Oh, how the game of assumptions is a deadly game. It has a way of "killing" relationships and marriages.

They finally pulled into the parking lot at Grace Mystery

Church and searched for a parking spot. They were late, so it was a little difficult to find one.

"Looks like we're gonna have to park out in the boonies today," stated David to himself as he pulled into a parking place that was furthest from the church's entrance.

Jessica just placed her black, leather purse in her lap and rolled her eyes, "We wouldn't have had to, if *someone* would get up earlier."

David's previous "reasoning" just worked to kindle their argument as he turned toward his wife in his seat, "Well, who was it that had to take fifteen minutes just to put some paint on her face?"

That really bit into Jessica, because she was "only doing it for him," but she didn't actually say that. She just puffed, grabbed her purse, and exited the car as swiftly as possible. Leonard could almost see the steam coming out her ears, though. And he was in the *back* seat.

After Jessica led the way, David just rolled his eyes and got out with everybody else. He joined his wife on the trek to the church's front door, but didn't think to grab her hand or anything. He just tucked his white, button-down shirt into his pants as the kids followed behind like pets on a leash. They didn't look like they could see where they were going, because they were looking down at their phones, but they somehow managed to make it to the front door.

Jessica saw them and gave them a glare as she let her parental authority fly, "Excuse me?! Put your phones away, we're at church."

They all reluctantly did as they were told and filed into the large foyer. The church's foyer had coat racks all the way down each side for all the coats that belonged to the church's many members. The coat rack line only ended on one side of the entryway to the auditorium, but then it started right back up again once the entryway ended. From where the Whittens were standing, the auditorium entryway was on the right wall and the hallway that led down to the large area for Sunday school classrooms was further down on the left wall.

Down the hallway to the Sunday school classrooms were the restrooms on the right side and the nurseries on the left side. As they all walked down the hallway, Jessica saw the colorful painting on the walls by the nursery doors and remembered when her father helped paint it. Her father had been an artist, but had died shortly after she married David. As she escorted Leonard to his classroom, she was taken back to when she was his age, going to the same classroom with the same teacher, except the teacher was younger back then.

The teacher was Mrs. Dorothy Duberry of now eighty-six years old. She was hunched over from lower back pain. Probably from all the kids she'd lifted in her days and had to rustle. She was a devout teacher of God's Word and stared you down through thick-lens, circular glasses. Her hair was short, gray, and curly. She spoke in the kindest old-lady voice you ever did hear, but, man, could she be firm when she wanted to. Leonard had gotten in trouble with her a few times before and suffered her wrath, but she still spoke kindly to him when she saw him coming in the doorway to her classroom. "Hello, Leonard! And how are you doing today, young man?!" She also had a tendency to yell, because of hard hearing, but she was still super sweet.

"Fine," was Leonard's simple and direct answer as he took a seat in one of the rows of short, orange chairs they were required to sit in.

Tanya Brooks waved at him, too, from her front row seat, but he didn't respond. You see, she was his Sunday school crush. She had long, brown curly hair and cute little freckles on her cheeks. She was a few years older than him, but wore the same style glasses.

When Leonard didn't respond, she just turned back around in her seat and looked down sadly as if her entire day had just been ruined by one action, or lack thereof.

Meanwhile, with the adults in the room, Jessica just smiled and nodded toward Mrs. Duberry, unwilling to carry on a conversation because they were late. Mrs. Duberry didn't care much either, because she wanted to start her class. She just smiled and waved, too. "Have a good day, honey!"

Eventually, everyone's Sunday school class started and the doors to the rooms were all closed. Leonard's class began with the normal singing that it usually does as Mrs. Duberry stood at the front of the class and directed. The first song they sang was "I'm in the Lord's Army," but then Leonard began to zone out. He appeared empty as he just sat down after singing and stared blankly at Mrs. Duberry moving her mouth. A lot was on his mind, especially the idea of being "in the Lord's Army."

"Am *I* in the Lord's Army?" wondered Leonard as he sat there, lifeless. Could he actually say, "yes, sir," and salute with certainty? It was a lot for a nine-year-old to handle, especially in his atmosphere at home. He hadn't really cared before, either, but it suddenly seemed important to him.

Dana and Matt were in the teen's class, being taught by Pastor Joe Harcan, their youth pastor. Pastor Joe looked like a middle-aged teenager with the way he styled his hair to look like a surfer, but you wouldn't find a nicer gentleman in the entire state. He was also quite good looking, but already taken.

Dana's attitude quickly changed as she entered the classroom doorway and saw Jennifer waving at her. She smiled and waved back as she tried to waddle over to the seat next to Jennifer in her tight dress. Matt just walked in with his hands in his pockets; arms flexed, and sat down in the closest seat he could find. Neither one of them ever brought a Bible. They were content to just make an "appearance."

David and Jessica naturally went to the adult class that was taught by their senior pastor, John Kathlin. Pastor John was gray-haired, but had it styled with a fringe haircut and his bangs parted centrally, hanging in the front. He was clean-shaven and had bright blue eyes. He looked quite nice for his age and spoke in a kind and gentle voice, but almost never smiled.

Everyone sat silently in their classrooms as they heard the Word taught to them. Well, everyone except the toddlers, that is. The toddler's class was taught by a twenty-one-year-old, blonde girl named Beth. She had bright, blue eyes, too, probably because she was Pastor John's daughter. Pastor John's wife, Clara, had died in childbearing, but thankfully, it was a girl that looked exactly like her. Whenever Pastor John saw his "little girl" wrangling the toddlers, he would just smile and see Clara in his daughter's place. It also caused him to be a little bit more protective over Beth, since she looked like her mom so much.

Beth tried to be a good role model for the other girls at church by dressing modestly and being patient in waiting for the right man to come along. Although, there was a new guy at church that had been eyeing her. Perhaps he could be the one? After all, this morning, he had volunteered to help her with the toddlers. She found herself a bit distracted by him and struggled to teach without smiling when he looked her way.

Eventually, after forty-five minutes of resituating yourself in your seat, the Sunday school classes were over and everyone filed out of the classrooms for the coffee break in the large area centrally located between all of the classrooms. They always got Schuler's homemade donuts for the coffee break, while one of their board members made his signature coffee.

The coffee break would last for about fifteen minutes and then the morning service would begin down the hallway in the large auditorium. The clock stroke ten-thirty and everyone washed down their last bit of donut with their last swig of coffee and headed for the auditorium. When they all arrived and prepared to sit down in the long, cushioned pews, Pastor John was already at the pulpit, surveying the territory. His eyes caught his daughter being escorted in by the "new guy," whose name just happened to be John, as well. Perhaps that's why Beth found herself attracted to him, because he reminded her of her first love, "Daddy."

Leonard made sure to sit in the furthest spot away from the end of the pew, because that's where his mother sat and he wanted to be able to play his game on his phone. It was called, "Immortal Empires." It was centered on a Chinese character named, Tang Lo, who could basically become the elements he touched and use them as a weapon. Chinese mythology played a big part in the game, as well, which is probably why Leonard was so into it.

You see, Jessica chose to make Leonard sit in on the main service and not go to junior church because he was old enough to sit under the pastor's in-depth teaching. A lot of good that did her, when he wasn't even paying attention past the announcements and opening prayer. He would just slouch back against the pew just far enough behind Matt's brawny body so that his mother couldn't see him and Matt sure wasn't about to make his little brother do what Mom said.

Leonard waited to put his ear buds in long enough to hear Pastor John say what the topic for the morning was, "Spiritual Warfare." He just smirked as he placed them in his ears and thought, "Lot o' that goin' around."

Everyone in the Whitten's pew was thinking that as they glanced at each other. Dana actually became interested in the message, for once. She sat next to her father with eyes fixed on the pulpit and ears awaiting the Truth she desperately needed to hear. Jessica began to feel tears build up in her eyes as Pastor John's message seemed to hit all the right buttons. David just nodded his head as he thought about the "Spiritual warfare" that had probably been going on during last night's little "temptation test." Matt just sat there, trying not to dose off, because the drugs he had taken gave him a massive headache that kept him up for most of the night.

Pastor John's words would penetrate Leonard's ear buds now and then. He would get just glimpses of his words as his hearing faded in and out, "You see, there is Spiritual warfare going on that we cannot see, because it is beyond our physical realm…Let's look at what the Word of God calls our adversary, because that's what the name 'Satan' means…He is called the Dragon many times. It is also said in Revelation 12:7 that he has angels that fight with him…He is also called the prince of the power of the air in Ephesians 2:2…But what's special about our God is that He is a triune God, a Trinity… He is God the Father, God the Son, which is Jesus Christ, and God the Holy Spirit or Ghost…Jesus Christ is called the Prince of Peace, so therefore we know we are to go to Him to find that peace in times of trouble and chaos…The only way to fight the Devil is to do what James 4:7 says, 'Submit yourselves therefore to God. Resist the devil, and he will flee from you.' We must take a strong stand in the Rock that we will not be moved, when the storm comes…" That was the last thing Leonard heard as his gaze was fixed on his Smartphone screen and a long, black-haired, Chinese man with mustache and goatee to match, punching and kicking his way across the planes with every command of Leonard's fingers. It fueled his young and unguided imagination as Tang Lo would turn a campfire into a blazing fireball, a sword into sharp and smooth cutting strokes of his arms, and strong punches by standing firm on the rocky ground.

Eventually, the service ended and everyone stood up for the closing prayer, but Leonard didn't notice. He just stayed sitting down, while everyone else stood up. This finally gave Jessica a chance to see that he wasn't paying attention. He looked up and his eye caught his mother's. He suddenly found himself swallowing hard and then jumping to his feet. Boy, did he know he was gonna get it. The inevitable boom was about to be lowered!

Leonard's ear buds were quickly pulled out of his ears and shoved in his pocket, along with his phone. He knew that wouldn't quench his mother's wrath, but it was worth a shot.

Everyone bowed their heads as Pastor John's soothing voice prayed, "Dear Lord in Heaven, thank you for this time we have been able to come before You and just soak in Your Word. I pray that You would be with us as we part ways from this place of worship and that You would help us to know and do Your will. Help us to use our gifts for Your glory," his right eye opened and he glanced at Leonard Whitten, before closing it again, "And I also pray that You would give us the strength and patience we need to go about our everyday tasks. In Jesus name I pray, amen."

With that, everyone began to file down the rows and then up the aisles to go out the large doorway to the auditorium. Pastor John always tried to rush to the doorway to greet people on the way out and made it there just in time to see the Whittens coming toward him. He smiled a little as he saw Jessica giving her youngest son the deadliest glare you ever did see. If looks could kill, Leonard would already be six feet under.

Pastor John shook each of their hands and when he got to Jessica, she felt the need to apologize as if she knew Pastor John had noticed Leonard, "I'm awfully sorry about Leonard, Pastor. It won't happen again."

Pastor John did his best to quiet the situation of "warfare" by smiling and roughing up Leonard's hair, "Oh, it's alright. He's just tuning up his God-given gift of imagination."

Jessica gave a fake smile and then quickly turned away as her face turned red, too. The Whittens quickly marched away as Pastor John watched sympathetically and muttered under his breath, "I just pray he doesn't waste it." He didn't realize it, but Leonard heard him and quickly glanced back around. Pastor John just stared at him and nodded toward him as if to say, "You know what I mean."

On the fifteen-minute drive home, every second was occupied with Jessica placing Leonard in front of the firing squad, "You know I don't like you playing on your phone during church and you deliberately sat as far away from me as possible! I don't care what Pastor John says! You were sneaky and I don't like it!" She threw her hands in the air and then seemed to clench some of it in a fist as she grinded her teeth together, "I just can't believe you would do that!" As you can see, she had quickly left off feeling sorry for herself. The chiding continued all the way home as David just sat silently in the driver's seat, letting his wife do all the work.

It didn't even seem to end after they got home and parted ways to their bedrooms. Jessica just kept right on spoutin' like an overflowin' fountain as she glared at David, "And why didn't you say anything?!"

David just shrugged his shoulders, "I didn't want to interrupt."

"Oh, well that's a good excuse not to involve yourself with your own family!"

"Hey! I'm the one that puts the food on the table and earns the cash around here!"

And so, the warfare just never seems to end. It even carried over to the lunch table as David cattily said to Leonard, "Your mother seems to want me to say something to you, son, so listen up…" He could already feel his wife's eyes burning a hole in the back of his head, because she was sitting on his left as he sat at the head of the table and Leonard was on his right. Dana sat next to Jessica, while Matt sat next to Leonard. It looked like boys versus girls with Dad as the referee, "It's important that you hear what Pastor John says, because he's a man of God…"

Jessica quickly felt the need to cut her husband off, "Oh, that's really profound!"

David just turned toward Jessica, "Would you like to handle this or can I do what *you* told me to?"

"Oh, so now you're blaming me?!" questioned Jessica as she pointed at herself.

"No, I'm not," stated David as he tried to remain calm by gripping handfuls of the laced tablecloth in his fists.

"Yes, you are!" disagreed Jessica as the children began to scrunch down in their seats. While further down the vittles plane, Dana and Matt had a fixed gaze on each other and were about to break out in another battle. Leonard just sat in his chair feeling rather uncomfortable. He already felt really bad for yesterday and this was just making it worse, so much so, that his eyes were about to burst with tears as the fighting kept getting louder and louder. Finally, he couldn't take it anymore and tears trickled down his face as he felt responsible for his parents' bickering.

Jessica suddenly held her fire and felt Leonard's tearful eyes burn into her heart, "Leonard, are you alright?" David stopped to look at his boy, too.

Leonard couldn't help but cry as he simply stood up and began running toward the staircase, while muttering through his tears, "I'm sorry." He ran up the stairs and they heard his door close above them.

Dana looked down from listening and began the shootin' again. She glared at Matt across the table and stated, "This is all *your* fault."

Matt raised his hands in innocence, if only he was. "How is it my fault?"

"*You* were sitting next to him and *you're* the one that encourages his stupid imagination!" Dana didn't know it, but Leonard heard her through the floor and began crying even harder. He now felt like everyone was against him, even his own sister.

"Well, *you* were right there, too! *You* could've said something!"

"I was actually focused on the sermon! I didn't notice Leonard! I was too busy feeling judged by what *you* said yesterday!" Dana violently thrust her finger across the table and pointed at Matt.

Matt just leaned in toward her finger, "Well, it's true!"

Dana withdrew her finger and became cocky, "Oh, you wanna talk about truth?! What if Mom and Dad knew the truth about you being addicted to pornography and doing drugs at Jack's house?!"

Now, even David was surprised as he placed his hands on the table and pushed away in shock, "Matt! Is this true?!"

Matt just pointed his guns at his father and continued pulling the trigger, "Well, what do you care?! You're always at work, anyway! The only time you *seem* to care about me is when I'm actin' like your perfect little clone!" With that, Matt threw his napkin on the table and marched upstairs.

David just sat in shocking thought, while Jessica turned to her daughter, "What did he say to you yesterday?"

Dana couldn't take it anymore either. She just removed herself from the battlefield, too, as tears began to flow, "I don't wanna talk about it." She finished her exit to her room and then Jessica turned to her husband, "Well, that's a fine mess you've gotten us into."

David came back to the land of the living and turned toward Jessica, "And how is this *my* fault?"

"Well, it can't be mine. I actually try to be here with the kids. *You* just spend all your time at the office, flirting with *Miss Cyndi Dunne!*"

David breathed heavily as he smoothed his hands over his bald head and then thrust himself up from the table.

"Where are you going?" asked Jessica quickly, as she watched her husband retreat.

David turned around toward her, "Well, since I spend so much time at the office already, I figured you could *assume!*" With that said, he left through the front door as Jessica stood up and rushed for the door as well. When she opened it, he was already out of the driveway. Tears filled her eyes as she walked down the driveway and cried, "Come back!" He turned the corner and she knew all hope was now gone as she fell to her knees. Matt watched from his window then sat down at his computer.

No one spoke to each other for the rest of the day. Everyone just stayed in their rooms, unwilling to enter the fray again. They didn't even eat supper that night. Leonard's conscience began to plague him again and he decided to open his door. He peaked out and saw the light on in the master bedroom down the hall. He snuck down the hallway past Dana's room and stopped by the master bedroom door that was cracked open just a little. He just stood there and listened to his mother cry her heart out before the Lord. She was on her knees at the foot of her bed as she cried, "God! Why is this happening?! Why?! Why am I not good enough?!"

Leonard suddenly felt a painful jolt inside of him as he continued to listen, "Why am I not good enough for my husband?! For my family?! Why am I not good enough for You?!" She continued to whimper as her face fell closer and closer to the floor, "What am I doing wrong?! Why won't you help me? Please help me! Please, God, help me!"

Leonard was now crying, too, as he walked away from his mother's door and back to his room. He shut his door and then fell on his knees, too. He looked up toward Heaven and simply prayed, "God? I've never done this before, but I know I need You right now. We all do. I don't know what to do, God. Please just show me. Please just teach me what I am to do. Please." There was a long pause and then he ended, "Amen." He got into his bed and suddenly found himself at peace as his head hit his soft pillow, quickly followed by the falling of his eyelids.

Meanwhile, Leonard's father wasn't experiencing that peace. His conscience had begun to weigh on him, but he didn't want to listen to it. He sat in his car in the office parking lot as he glanced out his driver's window and saw a sign for a bar. He used to be an alcoholic before he became a Christian. Back then, if he didn't want to feel something, he just drowned his feelings in booze. That sounded pretty good to him right now as he just continued to stare and then found himself starting his car and driving toward the establishment.

He was very slow to go in, but he did. As soon as he entered, he could hear the quirky, bar music and his eyes had to adjust to the dim-lit room. He felt the temptation come hard on him as he swallowed hard and rubbed his lips, watching other men down mugs of beer at the bar counter. He began to feel thirsty for what they had. His backside plopped on the bar stool and his arms fell onto the counter.

The bar tender looked at him and realized he hadn't ever seen him before. The bar tender had receding, brown hair that he combed straight back. He also had a full beard and mustache with a black and red, plaid shirt and blue jeans under his white apron. He was skinny and had his long sleeves rolled up his forearms. Needless to say, he looked like your everyday bar tender. He nodded toward David and asked, "You new around here?"

David looked up at the bar tender with fearful eyes as he swallowed hard, "Um, no. It's just my first time here…in a long time."

The bar tender nodded his head, "Ah, so what'll it be?"

For a split-second David stared at the men down the bar, just gluggin' down their beers, but found himself asking, "Could I have a water?"

He felt the temptation, he knew he shouldn't be there, and yet, he didn't leave. He just ordered water and continued to let himself be tempted by his surroundings. Strange how he knew exactly what to do when Cyndi Dunne tempted him, but right now, he didn't know what to do. It was a truly sad picture of a broken man.

Chapter Four
The Kingdom of Chaos

T he next time Leonard's eyes opened he was squinting at the bright sunlight that seemed to be shining between the leaves on a palm branch. He raised his right hand in front of his eyes as his vision cleared and saw that his hand looked much bigger and older than before. There were hairs sticking out of the back of his hand that hadn't been there when he went to sleep. As he looked up his arm from his hand, he realized he was wearing a black, leather bracer that came to a point just past his forearm. He rotated his arm and noticed that it was laced underneath.

As feeling came over his body, he felt a heavy warmth on his upper torso. He sat up and looked down at the rest of his attire. He was wearing a navy blue, wool poncho with black, leather bracers on each arm, dark gray pants, and black, leather knee boots. He tried to stand up by pushing up with his left arm, but something restricted him. He looked to the left of his belt and realized he was wearing a sword. With a puzzled look on his face, he just leaned back against the palm tree he was under and wondered, "Where in the world am I?" He looked back over his arms, "Who am I?" As he ran his hand over his face, he felt a full-grown beard and mustache. He quickly grabbed toward his hair and realized that it was rather long now. It came down to his shoulders and a strand from either side of his head seemed to be pulled around back and tied in a small knot to hold the rest of his pulled-back hair.

He had no mirror, so his sword would have to do. He quickly drew it and then began to turn it from side to side and gaze at his reflection. Amazement flowed over his face as he saw a reflection of a mature man with blonde hair. He looked rather handsome, too, I might add. With that, he gave a big grin and then sheathed his blade.

"Well, now what do I do?" asked Leonard out loud as he gazed at his surroundings that appeared to be nothing but desert far and wide.

Suddenly, he realized that he had just spoken in a deep, Australian accent.

"Am I in Australia?" Leonard wondered. "I've never been to Australia."

Suddenly, a Chinese voice came from his right and said, "You are in Bu Zing."

Leonard turned toward the voice and saw a middle-aged Chinese man staring at him. "Holy Moley! Where did you come from?"

The Chinese man appeared surprised, "Where did *I* come from? Where *you* come from dat make you use such strange words? I am Tang Lo." He pointed at himself.

Leonard suddenly appeared confused as he stared at this man that looked exactly like the main character from Immortal Empires and even had the same name, "Tang Lo? I know you…"

Tang Lo stood up straight as Leonard realized there were two other people standing behind him, "Strange, I do not know you."

Leonard just glanced between the three men that stood before him as he mumbled, "Well, I don't *actually* know you. I know *of* you." He was still amazed at this Chinese man that had the same characteristics as the videogame character. He even had the same graying temples, but yet his attire was a navy blue Gi and metal-plated bracers like Leonard's leather ones. He also wore the same style knee boots as Leonard and had the same style hair.

Finally, one of the men behind Tang Lo spoke up. It was the man on his right, who had long, black, wavy hair that hung loosely down to his shoulders and a big, black mustache decorated his upper lip. His skin was slightly pale and he wore a white, baggy-sleeved shirt with a black leather tunic wrapped over it all. A brown belt tightened the tunic to his body and held a rapier on the left side. The rest of the man's attire was black pants and knee boots. Everyone appeared to wear knee boots in "Bu Zing." The man leaned down toward Leonard and extended his right hand, "Hello, my name is Leviticus Helane, but most people just call me Levi." He spoke with a Spanish accent.

"Nice to meet you," stated Leonard as he shook Levi's hand and then Levi surprisingly pulled him up. Leonard wasn't expecting it and practically fell on top of Levi after he stood up, but he didn't because Levi was quick enough to let go. Leonard stumbled to get his footing as he tried to stand up straight and appear "older." His new acquaintances had no idea they were dealing with a nine-year-old in a grown man's body.

The man on Tang Lo's left was tall and brawny with red hair pulled back in a ponytail and a bushy, full beard and mustache. His attire was completely made of brown leather except for his bracers. They were rather blocky and seemingly made of wood. A brown, leather tunic covered his upper torso as loose-hanging, brown leather pants and knee boots covered his lower body. He did not appear to have any weapons like Tang Lo, and yet he did. He had a double-edged hatchet under each bracer. They appeared to be folded up in a mechanism that would explain the bracers bulkiness.

The brawny man clasped his right hand tightly on Leonard's surprisingly muscular forearm and stated in a deep, Russian accent, "I am Victor Vashti, vone of ze strongest men in Bu Zing."

After Leonard felt the crushing grasp of Victor Vashti, he could attest to that statement. "Ah, congratulations."

Suddenly, Tang Lo appeared frustrated as he jumped in front of their little "meet and greet" and began waving his arms about. "What are you doing?" He began to speak sarcastically as he dramatically mimicked them and smiled like a clown, "Hi, my name is Tang Lo. Welcome to Bu Zing! So happy to meet you!" His countenance quickly changed to a stern look as he continued, "Dis is Bu Zing, de Kingdom of Chaos. Dis is where everybody want to kill everybody!"

Leonard appeared confused as he pointed between them, "So why haven't *you* tried to kill me?"

Tang Lo shook his head as if awestruck that this masculine-looking man could be so dense, "Because I'm in de Lord's Army, duh!"

Leonard instantly saluted without realizing what he was doing and added, "Yes, *sir*!"

Tang Lo was now the confused one as Levi and Victor just laughed. Tang Lo squinted toward Leonard in confusion, "Why you just do dat?"

Leonard just held his right hand in thin air as he glanced around, unsure of what to do, "Uhhh, instinct."

"You very strange." Tang Lo began to turn on his heel to walk away when he turned back, waved his arm, and said, "Come along. You'll fit in quite nicely." Leonard eagerly followed his new companions.

Tang Lo led the way across the desert plane, while Levi and Victor each took a stand on either side of Leonard. As they marched through the desert sands, their boots and clothes became caked with dust. The wind began to blow the sands at them, as well.

After a little while of walking, Levi turned to Leonard and said, "So, where are you from, my friend?"

"Um, I'm just from Ohio," answered Leonard cautiously.

Victor decided to join the conversation as he turned toward Leonard in confusion, "Vat is zis 'Ohio'?" He flailed his hand about to demonstrate his confusion.

"Uhhh?" Leonard appeared unsure how to explain it and then he got an idea. He smiled and pointed at them, "It's round on both ends and high in the middle." He suddenly realized, after the fact, that this wasn't such a good description as Leonard's smile seemed to melt to a frown.

Levi seemed to understand, though, "Ah, so you are from the High Country? You are one of the Wise. That would explain why you are trekking across the Desert of Deception and sought rest under a palm tree."

Leonard was the confused one now. "What do you mean?" He had never heard of these places in geography at Reid Elementary.

Victor chose to explain this to his little friend. "Ze High Country is south from our position. Ve suppose zou are going to ze Greenlands, vhich is north of our location. Many of ze Vise are traveling across ze Desert of Deception to see ze vone called Christ. He is said to be very vise."

"But why is it called 'the Desert of Deception?'"

Tang Lo finally stopped the procession and turned around to explain everything to Leonard in one big bundle. "It is called de Desert of Deception, because de heat plays tricks on your senses deceiving you into tinking someting's dere, when it really isn't. It is also de domain of de Dragon, so we must hurry to de Oasis before dark." He turned back around and they began walking again, only faster now.

Leonard began to understand a little bit as what he had heard Pastor John say flashed into his memory, but then vanished. He still had many questions; after all, he was nine. "Why must we hurry?"

"Because the Dragon is the Prince of the Air." Levi waved his hand slowly upward and then brought it back down to continue. "He normally stays with the rest of the Rulers at the Citadel up north, but his Angels or Demons love to plague these parts with their deceptions because the Dragon's home is southeast of here. It is called the Enclave.

"You see, Bu Zing is the Kingdom of Chaos, because no Ruler has stayed on the Throne of the Citadel for more than one day. We are always fighting. We each belong to an Army and fight for its Ruler, while they just sit in the Throne Room, waiting to receive a message telling them the Throne is theirs. But there is one Ruler who actually fights alongside us. His name is Jesus Christ, the Prince of Peace. *He* must rule the Throne if we are ever to stop this endless chaos."

"I see," replied Leonard as he nodded his head. They continued their journey over the sand dunes, seemingly forever.

Eventually, they began to see palm trees in the distance and hoped the desert wasn't playing tricks on them, again. As they got closer, they saw the cool water spring at the center of the Oasis and were suddenly overjoyed. They began running for it, but then Tang Lo stopped right in front of them and they all bunched up like a comedy scene.

"Why have we stopped?" asked Leonard, desperate for water. He had never had to go this long without having some sort of liquid to pour down his throat.

"Because dere is someone already kneeling at de Oasis," answered Tang Lo as he squinted to try and see the figure, but it just appeared as a brown, blurry blob.

"I see him," added Levi as he drew his ever-ready blade and began to lead them toward the figure in the Oasis with it pointed in front of him.

The figure didn't even move until a blade was placed on his left shoulder. The figure was wearing all brown, except for a black belt and knee boots. His attire consisted of a capelet and hood with the hood up, a tunic with pants, and pieces of cloth wrapped up his forearm as if they were for bracers. He ever so slightly turned his head around and lowered his hood to reveal a face that looked exactly like Pastor John Kathlin. Well, except for the hair. It was still gray, but long enough that it was pulled around back in a small ponytail like Victor's.

"Greetings, brothers," said this look-alike of Pastor John as Levi appeared in awe and lowered his blade. With the blade removed from its striking position, the man stood up.

"Jonathan the Wise, we did not know it was you," stated Levi as he quickly sheathed his rapier and bowed.

Jonathan the Wise just smiled and used his hand to lift Levi's head. "No need to bow, my brother. I am not worthy of such glory that should only be given to the Trinity." He turned to each of them and nodded his head as if to say, "Hello," but when he came to Leonard, he paused and said, "I know all of these men, but I do not know you. Who are you?"

Victor was eager to answer for Leonard since Leonard was still in a daze from all Bu Zing had thrown at him. "Zis is Leonard ze Vise! He is vone of zou!"

"Is he?" questioned Jonathan the Wise as he thoughtfully squinted at Leonard.

Leonard finally decided to speak for himself and nodded his head. "Yes, I am from the High Country." He was beginning to "play along."

Jonathan the Wise nodded his head to show he understood, but still looked skeptical as he turned to Tang Lo and whispered, "Tell me, where did you find this man?"

"Under a palm tree in de mittle of de Desert of Deception between de High Country and here," answered Tang Lo appearing suspicious as he leaned in toward Jonathan the Wise.

"Well, he might just be a Demon in disguise…"

Tang Lo nodded his head to show he understood as he leaned away. "I will watch him *very* closely."

As night fell, they built a little fire near the spring and laid down around it as the wind's howling began to sound like screeching. Leonard was at first disturbed by it, but then he tried to ignore it by talking to his friend, Levi. "So, how are you all in the Lord's Army?"

Levi looked toward him, "What do you mean, my friend?"

"Well, um, you're all so different…" Leonard appeared to struggle to explain what he meant.

Levi smirked as he realized what Leonard was trying to say. "'There is neither Jew nor Greek, there is neither bond nor free, there is neither male nor female: for we are all one in Christ Jesus.'" (Gal. 3:28) Leonard began to understand from Levi's quote, but still he continued in a more joking manner, "Of course, there are those who take the 'neither male nor female' part a bit *too* seriously to the point of lusting toward familiar flesh that is not common nature. Them, we don't exactly know *what* Army they're in. They seem to have identity problems."

Leonard smirked a little at realizing what Levi was talking about, but then noticed Jonathan the Wise was staring at him again. Jonathan the Wise quickly looked away, but Leonard suddenly felt the need to create conversation with him now. "Jonathan the Wise?"

Jonathan the Wise looked back from leaning on his elbow to respond. "Yes, Leonard the Wise? What is it?"

Deep in thought, Leonard turned to stare into the fire and began to play with a weed on the ground, "Why do they call us 'the Wise'?"

Jonathan the Wise just smirked. "Those that live in the High Country are considered to be wise, because they are closer to the Trinity. The Trinity is God the Father, God the Son, and God the

Holy Spirit. It is said that God the Son is among us as the man Jesus Christ. He is also called the Prince of Peace and is said to be very wise. That is why I travel across the Desert of Deception to see for myself. I have greatly longed to see this Man." He looked at Leonard directly. "Why do you travel across the Desert of Deception, Leonard the Wise?"

Leonard suddenly felt uneasy as he peered into Jonathan the Wise's questioning eyes. He swallowed hard before he answered. "For the same reason. I long to see Him." He wasn't a very convincing liar.

Jonathan the Wise nodded his head, once again, but still didn't appear convinced.

With their conversation ended, Leonard could hear the screeching winds again. They began to frighten his little, nine-year-old mind as he seemed to curl up into a ball, forgetting he was a man. His imagination began to run rampant as he imagined what the screeching could belong to in this mysterious world.

Suddenly, it seemed to get so loud that all of the others started looking around. All at once, it stopped and the winds went still and the only sound was the rippling of the spring and crackling of the flames. Leonard began glancing around, completely frightened now, as his eyes caught something slithering down from a palm tree near the Oasis' edge. Victor saw it, too, and without a moment's hesitation, he leaped to his feet and flipped one of his double-headed hatchets into his hand. The blades unfolded as he gripped the handle in his raised right hand and then brought his arm swiftly down. The hatchet seemed to fly faster than light as it imbedded in the palm tree and chopped the head off of a snake.

The snake suddenly blew away in the wind like black dust and then the screeching began again. Leonard looked up and saw several beady, red eyes peering down at them. As they flew toward the light of the fire, he realized they were the ones screeching, because they were a fleet of Demons. Their faces were mauled and distorted along with the rest of their seemingly naked, pitch black bodies. Sharp, tattered wings stuck out of their backs and horns sprung up from their skulls. They grasped at you with withered arms and sharp claws as they growled and showed their fangs.

Some of the Demons landed near where Levi was now standing and he was rather eager to pull his blade. He slashed one of them across the face with his upstroke and the Demon stumbled backward and fell onto the fire. He screeched in horror as he seemed to turn to black dust and blow away in the wind, just like the snake before. These were definitely deceivers with their appearance, able to morph their bodies to look like anything, while being truly corrupt underneath.

With this act of aggression from Levi, the fight officially broke out because everyone seemed to start fighting at once. Levi continued to slice and stab with his rapier, while Victor chopped at the Demons with one of his hatchets, trying to make his way over to retrieve the other one. The air was suddenly filled with lots of black dust blowing around as the Demons were slain.

Victor suddenly became cornered and Tang Lo noticed his predicament, while Leonard and Jonathan the Wise just seemed to watch. Tang Lo punched and jabbed a few of the Demons, somehow making them turn to their black dust, and then jumped and twirled his body toward Victor's other hatchet. He landed with his right hand gripping the handle of the hatchet that was still wedged in the palm tree and tore it from its position and flung it across the battle grounds.

Victor just raised his empty right fist to pound one of the Demons and then his fist was suddenly filled with the handle to his missing hatchet. He didn't notice this until he brought the hatchet down and killed the Demon. He just glanced up, smiled at Tang Lo, and then roared toward another pack of Demons by the spring.

One Demon finally came at Jonathan the Wise. He flew down, grabbed him with his arms, and then began to fly back up again. Jonathan the Wise quickly grabbed the head of the Demon and twisted him into dust. In other words, he broke his neck and began freefalling toward the ground. He landed like a ninja with his hood up as he realized he was now in the middle of a pack of Demons. As they began to lunge at him, he would dodge and give them a death stroke with his surprising fighting ability.

Leonard appeared in awe at being able to actually live this battle scene, but then realized he had backed up against a tree. He stopped walking backward and looked to his right to see snarling fangs and flaming red eyes. His first instinct was to scream like a little girl and pull his sword, and he did. He followed through by jabbing it through the Demon's face who then blew away to dust.

Leonard suddenly felt the need to get away from the edge of the Oasis and rolled toward the fire as he stated, "These are just like zombies!"

Tang Lo heard him and paused for a second after taking out one of the Demons. With a look of confusion, he asked, "Who are dey?"

Leonard suddenly appeared geeky as he flung his blade about with a smile and replied, "Basically these guys, just without the wings."

Suddenly, Tang Lo appeared invigorated as he screamed, "Lookout!" He quickly stomped on the end of one of the fiery logs and it flipped upwards toward his awaiting hands. His hands seemed to rotate around the log as it floated in thin air. He quickly thrust his hands forward and a fireball shot toward the Demon that had come in behind Leonard. The fireball hit its target after Leonard dodged out of the way.

Leonard fell on his rump as he just stared at Tang Lo with mouth hanging open. "How'd you do that?"

All of the Demons were gone now, so Tang Lo broke his box

stance and stood normally as he replied with another question. "Do you not know de Arts?"

"Um, no," replied Leonard as Victor came over and helped him up. Victor had already replaced his hatchets into the bracers under his forearms.

Levi sheathed his blade as he frowned and asked, "Then what kind of Wiseman are you?"

"I don't know." Leonard looked down at his sword in thought as Jonathan the Wise just walked over with the familiar look of suspicion on his face.

Tang Lo decided to speak up and take charge. "Well, de sun will rise soon, so we should prepare to be on our way."

"I agree," stated Jonathan the Wise as he lowered his hood.

Leonard was suddenly curious again as he looked up and let his sword arm fall to his side. "That wasn't a very long night…"

Levi decided to clue-in this strangely dense Wiseman. "There has not been much time of darkness since Jesus Christ arrived in Bu Zing."

"Interesting," commented Leonard as he sheathed his sword as the sun suddenly began to rise behind him.

Tang Lo and Jonathan the Wise took to the lead, while the rest of them followed behind. After a while of marching, Leonard began to tire. He was not accustomed to such physical exertion. Not even tag at school was this tasking. "How much further until we reach the Greenlands?"

They just kept on walking as Jonathan the Wise simply replied, "We aren't going to the Greenlands."

Leonard appeared confused as his left hand rested on his sword's hilt and his other hand just flapped aimlessly at his side. "Then where are we going?"

Once again, Leonard's constant questioning caused the procession to come to a halt as its leaders both turned around.

Jonathan the Wise decided to answer, because Tang Lo was far too tired of Leonard's questions to respond calmly. "They are going to train you on the Bedrock at the Beach of Beauty, which is just northwest from where we are currently."

Levi placed his right hand on Leonard's left shoulder. "I am going to train you in swordsmanship."

Victor slapped his large, left hand on Leonard's right shoulder and nearly knocked him down. "And I vill train zou to use zour *fists*." He raised both his clenched fists into the air in typical brute fashion.

Tang Lo had finally calmed down enough to add his name to the list. "And I will train you in de Arts."

Leonard was quick to answer after hearing they were going to the beach and began waving his hands in front of himself. "Oh, no. I've seen enough 'beach beauty'. It's nothing but lust and... disturbing images." There was a pause, because he had a flashback of looking through his binoculars at the girls.

Jonathan the Wise just cocked his head and raised his eyebrows, "Is it? Or perhaps you are merely mistaken on what beauty truly is?"

They turned to keep walking as Leonard just stood dumbfounded and said, "Huh, perhaps..."

They began walking again, but Leonard felt the need to ask *just one more question*, "How are we supposed to train on the Bedrock with the regolith that's on top of it? It'll be too slippery."

They kept on walking despite his question. Jonathan the Wise just glanced behind with a smile and said, "You'll see."

Chapter Five
The Bedrock Trials

⁓⸙⸙⸙⁓

T he whole gang of soldiers journeyed on until Leonard began to hear the beautiful sound of waves crashing against a shore. There was now vibrant, green grass on the ground as they walked toward what looked like a giant bed of rock sticking out of a small ledge that led down to the shoreline. To their left was a large tree that cast shade over half of the Bedrock.

Levi turned around with a smile on his face and thrust his left hand in the air. "Welcome to the Beach of Beauty, Leonard the Wise!"

Leonard just smiled and nodded, because he was slightly taken aback that there were no women around to contribute to this "beauty." He began to wonder if he had been wrong about what true beauty was.

They all walked down the ledge and onto the sand. All of them ran to the water to throw some into their hot faces, except Jonathan the Wise and Leonard. Jonathan the Wise lowered his hood to feel the cool breeze from the ocean spray and then turned to Leonard with a fatherly smile. "Well, Leonard the Wise, does this meet with your definition of what beauty is?"

Leonard appeared to be gaping at this magnificent scene as he answered without turning his head, "I would have to admit that it far exceeds my expectations." He turned his head toward Jonathan the Wise with a look of confusion and said, "But there are no women?"

Jonathan the Wise just smirked as he turned back to watching the other men enjoy the cool water on their hot faces. "While women have to be one of the Trinity's most beautiful creations, they are not always needed for there to be beauty. Each piece of the Trinity's creation has its own aspect of beauty. It's just sometimes hidden beneath the surface, and *that's* when you know it's *true* beauty. Often true beauty is about what you *don't* see, not what you *do*."

"So that's why Jennifer looked more attractive in her one piece than the other girls did in their bikinis," thought Leonard to himself as he nodded his head. He thought a little bit more and then asked another question, "When is true beauty found in what you *do* see?"

Jonathan the Wise just smirked again. "When their actions show Godliness."

Leonard nodded his head, again, to show he finally understood what true beauty *really* is.

By now, the other men were done playing in the water and came back with it dripping from their faces and soaked facial hair. Leonard began to laugh at them as did Jonathan the Wise. Leonard decided to start some smack talk that he learned at school. "You look funny."

They just smiled as Tang Lo responded, "Well, it feel good."

That's not exactly what Leonard was expecting and it kind of took him off guard. He frowned slightly as Jonathan the Wise took the floor. He placed his hand on Leonard's shoulder, "Well, Leonard the Wise, I believe it is time to start your training."

Leonard just fake-smiled and nodded. He tried to act like he was alright as he rubbed his hands together, "Alright, who's first?"

Tang Lo got serious and jerked his head upward. "Dat would be me." He walked past Leonard and onto the Bedrock. He took a firm stance on the regolith and then waved Leonard to come up. "Come."

Leonard looked at Jonathan the Wise as if to ask what he should do and he just nodded his head toward Tang Lo. Leonard consented and went to walk past Jonathan the Wise, when he took a firm grip of his wool poncho and made him stop. Leonard looked him in the eye as he said, "You might want to remove this."

Leonard thoughtfully unwrapped the poncho from around his upper torso, dropped it on the ground, and stepped up on top of the Bedrock. His upper torso was now just covered by a dark, gray sleeveless shirt that exposed his masculine arms.

He slipped around a little on the regolith on his way toward Tang Lo, but managed to take a reasonable stand in front of him. They were standing right in the middle of the Bedrock with Leonard on the shaded side. Tang Lo pointed down at Leonard's sword with a stern look on his face and simply said, "Remove."

Leonard, once again, thoughtfully removed an object from his person and tossed it into the sand. He looked up and decided to go ahead and ask, "Why?"

Tang Lo was growing tired of Leonard's excessive questioning and rolled his eyes. He then leaned close into Leonard's face and annoyedly said, "Because you don't need it." It was like talking to a kid, probably because he was. He stood back up straight and continued in a more authoritative manner, "Now, take box stance."

Leonard just looked dumbfounded, "What's that?"

Tang Lo rolled his eyes, once again, and then explained, "You stand like dis." He raised his fists to his chest level and placed his feet in a diagonal position from each other.

Leonard somewhat understood, but still struggled to mimic Tang Lo's stance.

Tang Lo saw him struggling and broke his box stance to come stand on Leonard's right side under the shade. He patted Leonard's right leg and said, "Put dis leg in back, right corner of imaginary box on Bedrock." Leonard hesitated and then did as instructed. "Now, put left leg at top, left corner of box." Leonard, once again, did as instructed and was now standing in a box stance, so Tang Lo returned to his.

They were now standing across from each other and Leonard had finally gotten the idea and raised his fists. They were gonna fight. That's all Leonard thought he needed to know. He just smiled and then took a swing at Tang Lo.

When Tang Lo looked up from preparing his box stance, he had opened his mouth to start explaining the Arts, but instead, found a fist heading for his face. His instincts quickly kicked in and he had Leonard sitting on his butt within a few seconds.

Leonard's eyes got as large as watermelons as he felt his box stance be taken from underneath him and then it felt like a brick hit him in the chest. He had just experienced some firsthand use of the Arts. Tang Lo had turned his hands into the Bedrock just by reflex. He was kind of shocked as he realized what he had just done to his student. He quickly reached down to the gasping Leonard who sat at his feet. "Are you alright?"

Leonard could barely catch the wind that was just knocked out of him to respond. "I think so." He grabbed Tang Lo's extended hand and was pulled up. He wiped the dirt from his bum as he continued, "I think I just got my butt kicked within a few seconds of my first lesson." He turned to look at Tang Lo with a sheepish grin. "Not exactly the greatest start, huh?"

Tang Lo smiled, too, as he played along. "No, I would say not."

They chuckled a little bit more together and then returned to their box stances. Tang Lo got a serious look on his face, so Leonard could tell he was going to start teaching again. "Now, de Arts are very beneficial to know when it comes to war. Whatever you touch, you can become as long as you focus." That sounded simple enough, but Tang Lo didn't know he was speaking to a nine-year-old that lacked such a quality as focus. Tang Lo continued, "For instance, if you take firm foundation in rock, you will not be moved. But, if you take firm foundation in sand, you will easily be destroyed."

Leonard glanced between the Bedrock and the sand on the ground just to the left. He appeared to be understanding what Tang Lo was saying, so he continued, "I learned dat from Jesus Christ. When we reach de Greenlands, we shall take you to hear Him teach."

Leonard nodded his head. "I'd like that."

"Very well, let us begin again," stated Tang Lo as he took a firm box stance and Leonard did the same. Everyone watched in anticipation to see whether Leonard would kick Tang Lo's butt this time.

Even though Leonard had appeared to understand, it didn't seem to help much. He spent more time sprawled on the Bedrock than he did standing up, because Tang Lo was just too sleek and quick like a fox. Leonard slowly became more and more frustrated that he couldn't figure out what he was doing wrong and he was also getting more and more sore from hitting the Bedrock so many times.

Tang Lo saw the look of frustration on Leonard's face and tried to advise him to fix it. "You are big man, use it."

Leonard smiled and then glanced down at his flexing biceps, "Oh, yeah. I am a big man."

Tang Lo just slapped him and got in his face. "Excuse me, I was not suggesting arrogance."

That little baby slap didn't help. It just made Leonard angrier as he charged Tang Lo one last time and wound up on his back from a rather skillful flip from Tang Lo. Tang Lo just glanced down at

Leonard and said, "Never rush opponent." When Leonard stood up, he continued, "You also must remain calm under duress."

Leonard just wiped his mouth with the back of his hand and said, "You keep telling me what I need to do, but not letting me do it."

"No one else will give you a chance by taking it easy on you, so I will not." Tang Lo was trying to give Leonard a hard time, in hopes that he would show his true colors if he was a Demon in disguise.

Jonathan the Wise saw Leonard's face turning red with anger, so he decided to step in. "Perhaps it's time for Leonard to learn some swordplay?"

Levi smiled at the sound of that. Leonard wasn't exactly pleased and just glared at Tang Lo as he dismounted the Bedrock. Levi picked up Leonard's sword and tossed it to him, "You're going to need this, my friend."

Leonard surprisingly caught it with great precision. He appeared to have been focusing. Jonathan the Wise noticed it, but Tang Lo did not, because he had his back turned.

Levi unsheathed his blade and did a few quick slices and dices with it to get warmed up. Leonard tried to follow suit, but wound up cutting himself on his left hand and dropping his sword. Levi chuckled a little and then scooped Leonard's sword up with his right foot and tossed it back up to Leonard's hand. Leonard surprisingly caught it again as Levi began to train him in swordplay. "Now, my friend, you must take a firm stance like Tang Lo was speaking of and raise your blade up to cross with mine."

Levi got into position first and then Leonard was able to do the same. Their blades scraped against each other as they formed an "X" between the two of them.

"Now, when I swing my blade at you, simply place yours so that it will block mine. When I come down, raise yours horizontally above you," stated Levi as he swung down slowly at Leonard and he managed to block it, though his block was a little too high.

Levi saw this and advised him on it. "Oh, don't raise your blade too high, otherwise you will not be in a good position to defend against the next swing. Use quick, but slight movement, so that you'll always be ready.

"Now, I'm going to come at you from the side, so place your blade vertically to the left or right of you. Whichever way I come from." Levi swung at Leonard's left side at the same slow speed he had swung down at him. Leonard blocked it better this time with just a slight movement to his left, but not very quick.

Levi took a step back and smiled as he lowered his blade a little. "Very good, my friend. With a little practice, I think you will be just fine at swordplay." As you can see, Levi's training methods were a bit different than Tang Lo's directness.

They continued to train like this as their movements became quicker and quicker. All this time spent in this strange world and Leonard still had not had anything to eat or drink. He wondered if he ever would. The strange thing was that he really wasn't thirsty or hungry.

Suddenly, Leonard's thinking derailed his focus and Levi's swings came as a surprise to him. He blocked a few with his blade, but then tried to use his left bracer. He missed his mark and Levi's sword cut him just above the bracer.

"Ah!" cried Leonard in pain as he dropped his sword and reached for his forearm.

Levi could have kept swinging to show Leonard that you never want to let your guard down, even when you get hurt, but he didn't. He just took a step back and lowered his blade as he let Leonard bleed.

Leonard looked up at Levi with a look of surprise, as if he meant to do it. Leonard suddenly realized that no one was going to take it easy on him, because they all thought he was a grown man. He tried to act like a grown man or "big man" and fight like one, but that didn't really work. His idea of a grown man must have been off, because all he did was wind up with more cuts and bruises.

Levi began to feel bad for Leonard as he saw the bleeding cuts and blue bruised skin on his arms. He sheathed his blade and simply stated, "That's enough swordplay for today."

Leonard breathed heavily as he sheathed his sword as well and Levi stepped down from the Bedrock. Next, it was Victor's turn. Leonard was not looking forward to being beaten by this Russian brute. He just grimaced in annoyance as Victor mounted the Bedrock.

Leonard already knew he wouldn't need his sword for this training, so he threw it in the sand at Levi's feet. Levi felt a little disrespected, but didn't say anything.

Victor just gave a big smile and said, "Good! Zou know ve von't be using blades, but *fists!*" He thrust his in the air, once again.

Victor kept his fists raised and nodded his head for Leonard to do the same. Leonard just rolled his eyes and annoyedly raised his fists to a weak position that definitely was not a good idea. Victor just smiled and took a right cross swing at Leonard. Victor's fist connected with Leonard's jaw rather precisely and sent him to the Bedrock.

Victor just bellowed out a laugh as he put his fists on his hips and said, "Zou might vant to block, my little friend."

Leonard just rolled over, leaned up with one arm for support, and wiped his now bleeding lip with his other hand. He just stared at Victor with a look of disgust and then got an idea, when he saw Victor's open legs. This idea came from WWE.

Leonard quickly kicked Victor behind his left knee, which caused it to buckle a little, and then dove at his middle. Victor went to the Bedrock on his back with Leonard on top, but not for very long. Leonard's idea was good, but not good enough. Victor grabbed Leonard by the shoulders, placed his right foot in his middle, and then thrust him over himself. Leonard went flying off the Bedrock and you could almost hear the bell ring when he landed in the sand with a thud.

Victor stood up and began laughing, again, as Leonard lifted his head and spit out some sand with a large exhale. He had just gotten the wind knocked out of him, again, like when he was training with Tang Lo. Like any nine-year-old, he was getting tired of getting beaten all the time and never winning.

He quickly jumped up and shouted, "I'm done!" He stumped over to his sword, picked it up, and then went stumping away to walk along the Beach of Beauty's shore.

Victor was surprised and stopped laughing. Tang Lo went to chide Leonard, but Jonathan the Wise stopped him. "Let him go. I'll speak to him."

Chapter Six

Cross-training

About an hour past before Jonathan the Wise went looking for Leonard to talk to him. As he walked, he walked with his head down, following Leonard's footprints, until he came to a pile of objects. It was Leonard's sleeveless, bracers, boots, and sword. Jonathan the Wise looked up, when he heard splashing, and saw Leonard's head come up out of the water. Evidently, Leonard wanted to bathe to try and help his wounds.

Jonathan the Wise smiled and began walking toward where the waves splashed on the Beach of Beauty. Leonard saw him as a blurry image through the water on his eyelashes. He swam back to the shallow water and stood up as he rubbed his eyes. His bare upper torso broke through the water and it was a rather epic scene as he trudged toward Jonathan the Wise. His masculine, shirtless body was rather shiny and accented from the water as well as the cuts and bruises from his training. The intense look on his face made him look even more like a rather attractive man. His long, wet hair flapped about his face as he came toward Jonathan the Wise.

He stopped right in front of Jonathan the Wise as the water dripped from his face and body. He placed his hands on his hips, which just accentuated his muscles even more as he simply asked, "What are you doing here?"

Jonathan the Wise had to squint while he talked to Leonard, because the sun was so bright. In fact, they both did. "I came to discuss some things with you."

Leonard walked over to his effects. "Oh yeah? And what's that?" There was nothing to dry himself off with, so he just went ahead and put back on his sleeveless, but didn't tuck it in.

"Why are you so easily defeated?" asked Jonathan the Wise with a bit of hesitancy.

Leonard just smirked as he began to fasten his bracers back on. "Huh, that's amusing." He turned back around toward Jonathan the Wise. "Perhaps it's because I'm just not good enough to be in the Lord's Army."

Jonathan the Wise got a rather serious look on his face. "You don't mean that."

Leonard was surprised at Jonathan the Wise's boldness and showed it with a puff and cock of his head. "Oh, then what *do* I mean?"

Jonathan the Wise stepped closer to Leonard. "I believe your wounds go deeper than just the surface. They are wounds that I cannot see with my eyes, but I hear them with my ears. Your voice speaks volumes of your inner pain, young one."

Leonard had been looking down, putting his boots back on, when he heard what Jonathan the Wise called him, and quickly looked up, "Why'd you just call me that?"

"Because you might be a grown man on the outside, but your inner wisdom is like that of a youth. You are one of the Wise, but still have lots of room to grow."

Leonard slipped on his last boot and then lifted his sword to his belt. He sheathed it thoughtfully as he spoke, "You are rather correct on that account, Jonathan the Wise." He was just thankful that he wasn't completely exposed as to who he *really* was.

"Thank you. I will not tell the others. You see, we have been cautious toward you, because we thought you might be a Demon in disguise. You are in disguise, Leonard the Wise, but not because you are a Demon. But because you are truly young to the Trinity. You are afraid to show it, because of your shame." Jonathan the Wise began shaking his head, "Don't be."

Leonard just glanced around in an awkward fashion as Jonathan the Wise spoke. He then asked, "So, what are *you* going to train me in."

Jonathan the Wise smirked, "I'm doing it right now."

Leonard smiled, too. "What do you mean?"

Jonathan the Wise tilted his head to one side as he said, "Why do you think you keep losing?"

"Because I can't beat them at their own game."

Jonathan the Wise smiled, "So, beat them at someone else's game."

"What do you mean by *that*?"

Jonathan the Wise swallowed and then acted like he was about to give a sermon. That's how Leonard was used to seeing him, so he didn't mind. "If you can't beat Tang Lo in the Arts, beat him in fist fighting or swordplay. If you can't beat Levi at swordplay, beat him in the Arts or fist fighting. If you can't beat Victor in fist fighting, beat him in the Arts or swordplay."

Leonard began to understand as he said, "Ahhhh, so you want me to trick them by using other people's techniques?"

Jonathan the Wise smiled and nodded his head, "That's precisely right. It's called cross-training. By themselves, each aspect of your training is useless to you, but if you combine them, they become invaluable to you."

Leonard smiled, too. "Thank you, Jonathan the Wise. You've given me hope for tomorrow."

Jonathan the Wise shook his head, "I did not give you hope. The Trinity did. He is the supplier of everything. You'll learn that soon enough." He placed his hand on Leonard's shoulder and began to lead him forward. "Come. Let's go back to the Bedrock."

When they finally got back to the Bedrock, it was dark and the others had made a campfire with twigs from the large tree by the Bedrock. They didn't say much to each other as they lay around it, preparing to sleep through the short night. Apparently, no one ate in Bu Zing.

Leonard fell asleep on his wool poncho, listening to the gentle sound of the waves hitting the shore of the Beach of Beauty and the pleasant crackling of the campfire. He had bright hopes for tomorrow's day of training on the Bedrock as everything was just starting to make sense.

As before, it was a short night, but Leonard didn't mind because he was anxious to start the next day of training. He already had planned how he was going to "mix it up." Boy, were *they* in for a surprise...

When the sun started to rise, Leonard was the first to rise with it. Jonathan the Wise was slightly surprised as was everyone else. Tang Lo smiled and playfully asked Leonard, "Anxious to get your butt kicked, again?"

Leonard just smiled, too, and tilted his head. "Oh, we'll see whose butt gets kicked today, my friend."

Tang Lo stepped up onto the Bedrock as he wondered what Jonathan the Wise had said that made Leonard so confident all the sudden. He stopped in the middle where they were before and then waved his hand for Leonard to join him. "If you so confident, get you butt up here." He was back to his old, direct self.

Leonard just kept smiling as he mounted the Bedrock. Tang Lo was no longer smiling, though. They began to circle each other as Tang Lo stated, "Smiling insinuates arrogance."

Leonard still didn't stop smiling. "No. I'm just going to have a lot of fun." He pulled his sword out to toss it away, but touched the blade with his hand before doing it. Tang Lo saw his eyes light up and instantly realized what he was doing.

Leonard threw his sword into the sand and then poised his hands at his chest, but did not close them to make a fist. He just kept them ready as if he was going to perform a karate chop.

With this evidence, Tang Lo acted. He was not going to take it easy on Leonard, who obviously had been listening to how to use the Arts. But what Tang Lo did not expect was for him to combine swordplay with the Arts.

Tang Lo turned himself into the Bedrock and began kicking and punching at Leonard with great speed. Leonard just blocked and returned with a swing of his own. When he would block Tang Lo's blows with his arms, it would cause sparks to fly, because that's what happens when metal scrapes rock.

At first, Tang Lo seemed to be forcing Leonard back like before, but when Tang Lo went for a knockdown blow, Leonard ducked and then tripped him. He stumbled backward and lost focus so that he was no longer the Bedrock. Leonard took this opportune moment to start pushing *him* back. He swung at Tang Lo with his sword-like arms as Tang Lo resorted to doing nothing but blocking them with his metal-plated bracers. He did not have time to refocus on the Bedrock.

Tang Lo kept up with Leonard's swings and all you could hear was a chinking sound of metal hitting metal each time Leonard's arms connected with Tang Lo's bracers. Eventually, Leonard became so confident he began doing flips and leaps all over the Bedrock to keep Tang Lo off balance. And, boy, did he succeed.

Tang Lo was now pinned against the edge of the Bedrock

and fighting for his life, in a sense. His foot slipped off and he lost concentration, so that he tried to block Leonard's arm with a right, palm-heel strike. Instead, his hand was cut and he grabbed at it in pain, "Ah!"

Leonard took advantage of Tang Lo's lowered defenses and quickly turned himself into the Bedrock and kicked him in the chest. He went flying off the Bedrock and landed with a thud in the sand. He lay there for a little while and then coughed out a few breaths as he began to realize how Leonard had felt the day before.

This whole time, Jonathan the Wise had just been smiling, while the other two trainers stood in amazement.

Tang Lo sat up and looked at Leonard with a grimace that then turned to a rough smile. "Good job. You did not take it easy on me."

Leonard just flashed his grin, again, as he jumped down to help his fallen trainer up. "Thank you."

Tang Lo was hesitant to grab his hand, but then realized it couldn't be a blade anymore. He walked over to the others to join Levi, who was hesitant to step onto the Bedrock, after seeing Leonard's performance in the Arts.

Eventually, Leonard joined Levi on the Bedrock with the same smile he had before. Levi drew his sword as did Leonard and then Levi began to toy with him to see what he would do. Levi smiled a little, too, as he began to push Leonard back into the shaded area.

Leonard continued to back up around the Bedrock, turning now and then, so that he wouldn't be pinned against the side. He didn't seem to be going to change his arms into swords this time. He was actually doing fairly well by just using swordplay. Levi's kinder methods of training appeared to have had a better effect on him, so that he actually caught on.

For a while, they just dueled about the Bedrock, sidestepping, lunging, and blocking all the time. Then, Levi got Leonard off balance and managed to twist his blade around Leonard's many times and then prick it out of his hand. It clanked on the Bedrock as Levi thrust his blade's point at Leonard's head. He dodged to the right and grabbed the blade by sandwiching it between his two palms. His eyes lit up and that tended to frighten Levi as to what he would do next.

Leonard took Levi's sword from him and threw it over his shoulder. Levi finally came back to his senses and tripped Leonard, so he fell to the right. He stumbled a little bit and then took a firm stance on the Bedrock. His eyes glowed, once again, and he spun around with his right arm extended.

He clothes-lined Levi as he was running for his sword. Levi's lower body tried to keep going as his upper torso stayed latched onto Leonard's steadfast arm and he fell onto the Bedrock. You heard a thud and then a deep exhale, followed by a groan.

Leonard just hunched over Levi with a smile as he tried to retrieve his breath. Once he did, he looked up with a frown and asked, "Who taught you to combine your training?"

Leonard helped Levi up as he answered, "Let's just say it's a quality among the Wise." He turned to Jonathan the Wise and winked. Jonathan the Wise just nodded and smiled in return.

Levi proceeded to pick up his sword and sheath it on his way off the Bedrock.

Victor had seen both fights before him and felt prepared to face this young amateur. He smiled widely as Leonard and he raised their fists.

Once again, Leonard let himself be backed up as he kept dodging Victor's swings. Eventually, Victor stopped smiling and grew tired of missing Leonard's smiling face. You might even say he became frustrated, because Leonard wasn't even throwing any punches of his own.

Suddenly, Leonard was against the edge and Victor bull-rushed him. Leonard just dodged to the side and stuck his foot out. Victor went flying off the Bedrock and into the sand. Leonard had realized that this brutish of a man only liked fist fighting because of the physical contact. So, if there was no physical contact, he would grow tired of the fight and then Leonard could use his own frustration or strength against him.

Well, Victor was not so easily beaten. He just wiped the sand from his face and climbed back onto the Bedrock. Leonard hadn't begun to celebrate just yet, either. They began circling each other again with their fists raised and ready.

Suddenly, they stopped circling with Victor in the shaded area and then they both took a box stance. Victor took a hard swing at Leonard and he just dodged to the right as his eyes glowed. Victor saw his eyes glow and knew what that meant. A hard, left jab that felt like a rock hitting him in the face connected with Victor's jaw and then it was followed by a right cross that dazed him. He stumbled backward a little and then saw Leonard winding up for a kick. "Oh, no."

Leonard pulled his arms behind his body to give the kick more power and then snapped his right foot toward Victor. The kick connected with Victor's chest and sent him flying backward like a rocket. He slammed into the large tree and snapped it in two. It began to fall on top of him, but then Leonard stood underneath it in his rock-like self and held it up with his raised hands.

Tang Lo and Levi helped Victor from under the tree and then Leonard dropped it. Jonathan the Wise smiled with great pride in how much "young Leonard" had grown. Tang Lo just switched his gaze from the delirious Victor to Leonard and stated, "You are ready to be in de Lord's Army, now."

Leonard just smiled and saluted, "Yes, sir."

Chapter Seven
Sitting in the Citadel

When Victor finally recuperated from Leonard's knockdown, they began their journey toward the Greenlands. It was about mid-day when they started their trek. They began to walk, when, all of the sudden, Leonard's vision flashed black and then flashed to an entirely different area. It was like his spirit was floating around and he was now in a large room filled with different people sitting in chairs. They spoke amongst themselves as Leonard began to look around.

The room was all made of stone and there was a large archway on his left that led to a shadowy tunnel he couldn't see down. It was just all black. He seemed to float closer to the group of people, but no one noticed him as if he was invisible. The closer he looked at the people, the more he realized they were the Rulers Levi had mentioned. They all sat on thrones with red cushions and gold molding around the cushions, arms, and legs.

From left to right, you could tell exactly who they were. First was unmistakably Napoleon Bonaparte with his bicorn hat. Second was Ramses, Pharaoh of Egypt, who just looked like Yul Brynner from the Ten Commandments. Next was the large, center Throne that no one occupied until they were informed who was the current Ruler on the Throne, which was based on the outcome of the battle of the Armies. Beside the central Throne was Queen Victoria of England, who strangely looked like Miss Abigail Scotts. That was rather amusing to Leonard as she was his elementary school teacher and her last name was Scotts.

Next, was Adolf Hitler, who looked like Leonard's principle, Mr. Thomas Crank. It just looked like him with Hitler's famous mustache, that is. The interesting thing was, these were basically all the people Leonard had been learning about in history at school.

Leonard began to hear what they were saying as Hitler stood up and began to pace with his hands cupped behind his back and his chest thrown forward. "Vere is ze Dragon?! He is alvays late! *He's* ze vone who called for zis meeting to be held in ze *first* place!"

Napoleon piped up and Leonard turned to him. "Oui, oui. I mean he has wings. It couldn't *possibly* take zat long to fly here from zat Enclave of his. What was he doing zere, anyway? He's supposed to be here."

Ramses decided to join in as he sat calmly on his throne. "He spends much time there in preparation for killing the One calling Himself Christ. *That* is probably what he wants to talk about."

Queen Victoria just sat cool-headedly, just like Miss Scotts would, as the disputing went on around her. Once it was over, then she would calmly say what needed to be said, but a sound from the dark tunnel kept her from doing just that. It sounded like large footsteps as the whole room shook. Little pebbles fell from the ceiling, right where Leonard would be, but when he thought to raise his arms to shield himself, the pebbles seemed to fall right through him. He looked down and saw no physical form. He *was* invisible.

Suddenly, giant red eyes began to glow through the darkness of the tunnel, but that's all Leonard could see. He felt a chill go up his spine as he realized that it was the Dragon. A deep and chilling voice came from the darkness as you began to hear purring, as well, "I *did* call for this meeting in order to talk about the death of the One called Christ. I have finished preparations for the death of the Prince of Peace."

"But why should He be killed?" asked Queen Victoria as she was finally able to speak after the shock and fear at the Dragon's appearance.

"That's just what Miss Scotts would say," thought Leonard as he looked back toward the glowing eyes of the Dragon.

A violent puff of air came from the Dragon's gigantic nostrils and blew the tapestries that hung on the opposite wall, as well as caused Hitler to have to sit back down. Leonard also saw dust shoot across the floor and took a deep breath as he wondered just how big the Dragon was. "Because he thinks Himself better than us. He thinks that because He's willing to fight alongside His soldiers, He's *stronger* than us."

Hitler began to speak from his now sitting position. "And how do zou know all zhis?"

The Dragon sounded furious as he replied, "Have you not heard his treacherous teachings?!" The blast from his speech blew across the room, again causing a great tempest in its structure.

Ramses just sat straight up and said, "No, but apparently *you* have. Care to explain how?"

Suddenly, a giant, black, scaled foot came piercing through the darkness of the tunnel and hit the floor. It created a crater beneath its blow as giant, sharp claws dug into the stone, causing great, deep cracks. A roar came at the same time as the blow and everything went silent as everyone leaned back in their thrones in shock. You could only hear the loud, angry puffs of breath from the Dragon's nostrils.

After glancing around at the other Rulers cowering in their

thrones, the Dragon slowly retracted his claws back into his foot. They made a horrible scraping sound as they came out of the holes they had made in the stone. He withdrew his foot back into the darkness and simply stated, "I have watched from afar."

Everyone relaxed, including Leonard, whose heart had been pounding vigorously since the Dragon first entered.

Queen Victoria sat forward in her throne. "And what do you propose we do, Dragon?"

The Dragon's black pupils went thin as he stared at the Rulers intently. "Crucify Him."

Shock went throughout the room, once again, as you heard gasps that sounded like everyone was trying to catch their breath. Leonard was shocked, as well.

Hitler was the first to speak. "It shall be done. Tomorrow is ze battle of ze Armies. Zou shall crucify Him if He manages to live through it."

"I will perform the crucifixion at the Enclave," stated the Dragon, his smile being heard because his scales rubbed together with the movement of his lips.

"Agreed," said everyone at the same time. Queen Victoria was a bit hesitant, though.

The Dragon's eyes disappeared in the darkness and then Leonard heard giant wings flapping, again. He didn't know why, but the knowledge of what had just been decided weighed on him. His conscience was at work, again, and he felt the sudden urge to warn the One called Christ.

Chapter Eight

The Storyteller

~※※※~

Suddenly, Leonard's vision flashed, again, and he was now standing in a field of vibrant, green grass blowing in the soft breeze. It was bright and sunny out, so he had to shade his eyes with his hand to see more of his surroundings. As he focused, he saw hundreds of people gathered in front of him, but he didn't see any of his old friends. He began to wander toward the crowd as he began to hear a soothing voice speaking to the multitude of listeners.

He suddenly saw the back of someone that somehow looked familiar. It was a girl with long, brown hair and she was wearing some rather beautiful and majestic silver armor. On the back of her armor was a phoenix and then a cross on each of her metal bracers. A sword hung on the back of her armor diagonally. Beneath her armor was some simple, tan, wool clothing. She began to feel someone watching her and gave a quick glance behind her before turning back around.

Leonard gasped as he realized that it was his Sunday school crush, Tanya Brooks. She was all grown-up-looking like him, of course, but he could still recognize her deep, brown eyes and cute freckles on her cheeks. He instantly smiled, but she didn't notice him. He was rather pleased with himself when he remembered how good he looked in his new body. He paraded over to her to strike up some conversation. "Hello there."

Tanya turned around and saw him. Her first thought was that he *did* look handsome, but then she remembered Jesus was teaching. She politely said, "Hello." She turned back toward Jesus as he stood in the center of the people.

Leonard was a bit disappointed as his smile faded and then he looked toward where she was looking. He saw someone that was clearly a man wearing a white, wool robe with a red sash hanging diagonally across his upper torso. He couldn't see his face, though. When he would try to focus on His face, it would just become all pixelated and blurry.

Leonard felt the need to ask a pretty obvious question, but that's just because he wanted to be sure of what he was or wasn't seeing. "What's going on?"

Tanya replied, but still kept her eyes on Jesus, "Our Ruler, the Prince of Peace, is teaching us today. He's preparing us for the battle of the Armies tomorrow."

"Oh," said Leonard as he slowly raised his head and then lowered it in a sort of bored fashion.

He began to look around, again, at all the people and saw Jonathan the Wise. He moved over next to him and gave no greeting before asking, "Is that the One called Christ?"

Jonathan the Wise was sort of startled, but then smiled when he saw who it was that asked him the question. "Yes, that's Jesus Christ."

Leonard kept squinting and trying to get a better angle as he asked, "What does He look like? I can't see His face."

Jonathan the Wise looked thoughtful as he glanced between Leonard and Jesus. "Perhaps, you cannot *see* Him, because you do not yet *know* Him?"

Leonard was at first confused, but then realized Jonathan the Wise was speaking his very thoughts that had been bouncing around in his head since they sang "I'm in the Lord's Army" in Sunday school. He became very quiet and distant as he began to listen to Jesus teach, too.

Jesus paced in front of them, often lifting His hands in a beckoning sort of manner as he taught, "Once, 'a sower went out to sow his seed: and as he sowed, some fell by the way side; and it was trodden down, and the fowls of the air devoured it. And some fell upon a rock; and as soon as it was sprung up, it withered away, because it lacked moisture. And some fell among thorns; and the thorns sprang up with it, and choked it. And other fell on good ground, and sprang up, and bare fruit an hundredfold.'" (Luke 8:5-8a)

He appeared to take a breath and look around at the people's confused faces. Leonard was definitely confused, but that's why He continued to explain his story. "Now, 'the seed is the Word of God. Those by the way side are they that hear; then cometh the Devil, and taketh away the Word out of their hearts, lest they should believe and be saved.'" (Luke 8:11b-12) Leonard became very interested in what Jesus was saying.

"'They on the rock are they, which, when they hear, receive the Word with joy; and these have no root, which for a while believe, and in time of temptation fall away. And that which fell among thorns are they, which, when they have heard, go forth, and are choked with cares and riches and pleasures of this life, and bring no fruit to perfection.'" (Luke 8:13-14) Leonard felt very guilty as every word that proceeded out of His mouth seemed to cut to his heart.

"'But that on the good ground are they, which in an honest and good heart, having heard the Word, keep it, and bring forth fruit with patience.' Now I challenge you, which seed are you?" (Luke 8:15)

Leonard felt extremely touched by His teaching, but thought, "Well, I'm certainly not the good seed. I'm just not as good as

Tanya. She probably doesn't sin at all. She's in the Lord's Army for sure, but I'm not." Tears swelled in Leonard's eyes as he realized his depravity.

Jesus appeared to look directly at him as He continued to teach, "Some of you will think yourselves not good enough and compare yourselves with others, but listen well, all of you. 'The Kingdom of Heaven is like unto a man that is an householder, which went out early in the morning to hire laborers into his vineyard. And when he had agreed with the laborers for a penny a day, he sent them into his vineyard. And he went about the third hour, and saw others standing idle in the marketplace, and said unto them; 'Go ye also into the vineyard, and whatsoever is right I will give you.' And they went their way.

"'Again he went out about the sixth and ninth hour, and did likewise. And about the eleventh hour he went out, and found others idle, and saith unto them, 'Why stand ye here all the day idle?' They say unto him, 'Because no man hath hired us.' He saith unto them, 'Go ye also into the vineyard; and whatsoever is right, that shall ye receive.'

"'So when even was come, the Lord of the vineyard saith unto his steward, 'Call the laborers, and give them their hire, beginning from the last unto the first.' And when they came that were hired about the eleventh hour, they received every man a penny. But when the first came, they supposed that they should have received more; and they likewise received every man a penny. And when they had received it, they murmured against the goodman of the house, saying, 'These last have wrought but one hour, and thou hast made them equal unto us, which have borne the burden and heat of the day.'

"'But he answered one of them, and said, 'Friend, I do thee no wrong: didst not thou agree with me for a penny? Take that thine is, and go thy way: I will give unto this last, even as unto thee. Is it not lawful for me to do what I will with mine own? Is thine eye evil, because I am good?' So the last shall be first, and the first last: for many be called, but few chosen.'" (Matt. 20:1-16)

Leonard felt somewhat relieved by what Jesus had said, but still thought, "I've done too much wrong to be in the Lord's Army."

Once again, Jesus heard his thoughts and spoke up, "A certain man had two sons: and the younger of them said to his father, 'Father, give me the portion of goods that falleth to me.' And he divided unto them his living. And not many days after the younger son gathered all together, and took his journey into a far country, and there wasted his substance with riotous living. And when he had spent all, there arose a mighty famine in that land; and he began to be in want.

"'And he went and joined himself to a citizen of that country; and he sent him into his fields to feed swine. And he would fain have filled his belly with the husks that the swine did eat: and no man gave unto him.

"'And when he came to himself, he said, 'How many hired servants of my father's have bread enough and to spare, and I perish with hunger! I will arise and go to my father, and will say unto him,' 'Father, I have sinned against Heaven, and before thee, and am no more worthy to be called thy son: make me as one of thy hired servants.'

"'And he arose, and came to his father. But when he was yet a great way off, his father saw him, and had compassion, and ran, and fell on his neck, and kissed him. And the son said unto him, 'Father, I have sinned against Heaven, and in thy sight, and am no more worthy to be called thy son.'

"'But the father said to his servants, 'Bring forth the best robe, and put it on him; and put a ring on his hand, and shoes on his feet: and bring hither the fatted calf, and kill it; and let us eat, and be merry: for this my son was dead, and is alive again; he was lost, and is found.' And they began to be merry.

"'Now his elder son was in the field: and as he came and drew nigh to the house, he heard music and dancing. And he called one of the servants, and asked what these things meant. And he said unto him, 'Thy brother is come; and thy father hath killed the fatted calf, because he hath received him safe and sound.' And he was angry, and would not go in: therefore came his father out, and entreated him. And he answering said to his father, 'Lo, these many years do I serve thee, neither transgressed I at any time thy commandment: and yet thou never gavest me a kid, that I might make merry with my friends: but as soon as this thy son was come, which hath devoured thy living with harlots, thou hast killed for him the fatted calf.'

"'And he said unto him, 'Son, thou art ever with me, and all that I have is thine. It was meet that we should make merry, and be glad: for this thy brother was dead, and is alive again; and was lost, and is found.'" (Luke 15:11-32)

Leonard suddenly felt like a hammer had just clubbed him in the head as everything began making sense. Jesus continued to explain, "You see, dear ones, you are never too far gone that I cannot bring you back again. You have never done too much wrong that I cannot forgive. You are never out of the reach of the Trinity. He's always been waiting at your door."

Leonard felt a sense of comfort from Jesus' teachings and sort of relaxed his shoulders and smiled. He was now on the path to salvation, having understood the darkness and depravity of man. Next, he would need to learn that he can't do it on his own...

Chapter Nine
Let My People Go

⁓※⁂⁓

That night, Leonard couldn't stop thinking about what Jesus had said. He was so lost in thought as they all sat in groups around different fire pits in the grassy field. Jonathan the Wise was with Leonard at one and noticed his absent-mindedness. He scooted over to him and asked, "What is the matter, Leonard the Wise? You appear lost?"

Without even thinking or making any hint of movement, Leonard responded, "That's because I am." He glanced up and saw the look of shock on Jonathan the Wise's face, so he continued with the sincerest voice you ever did hear, "I'm lost, Jonathan the Wise. I'm not in the Lord's Army, and I'm not a grown man."

Jonathan the Wise smiled and thought he was talking about what he said at the Beach of Beauty. "Are you referring to what I said about you being a young Wiseman?"

Leonard began shaking his head. "No. *I am* just a boy in a man's body." Jonathan the Wise stopped smiling. "I don't know why I'm here, but I *and* my family are lost." His voice quivered as he spoke.

Jonathan the Wise looked very thoughtful as he stated, "You and your family are not lost."

"How do you know?"

"Because no one's ever really lost until they've passed on in unbelief. They are never too far gone in this life, dear friend. The Dragon's hold on you and your family is strong, but the Trinity is powerful."

Leonard looked up with a frown. "What do you mean, 'the Dragon's hold?'"

Jonathan the Wise situated himself comfortably on the grass and began to explain, while leaning on his side. "Everyone has a choice to do right or wrong, but the sad thing is that man is naturally prone to choose wrong. Thus, they choose to let the Dragon have a hold on their lives, and the more you choose to do wrong, the stronger that hold becomes. You must be pried from the Dragon's hold, before it is too late."

Leonard was hesitant to ask, but asked anyway, "When is it too late?"

"When the wages of sin come," was Jonathan the Wise's simple answer.

Leonard looked back down at the fire as he felt one kindling inside of him. It was anger and hate for the Dragon. The fire gleamed in his eyes as he clenched a tight fist about his sword's hilt and plotted how to slay the Dragon, "I will go to the Enclave while everyone sleeps. It won't take long." His jaw flexed and his hand twisted tightly back and forth on his sword's hilt as he continued to think, "I'll give him a quick death. I wish I could prolong his agony like he's done to me, but there isn't time."

Suddenly, they heard a loud boom in the distance that sounded like a thunderstorm. Leonard didn't remember hearing it on previous nights and asked Jonathan the Wise, "What is that? It sounds like a thunderstorm."

"It is one. There is often a storm brewing above the Enclave. It is a dark place and the home of the Dragon and his Demons. It is a great distance from here." Jonathan the Wise looked at Leonard suspiciously, "I'm surprised you can hear it."

Leonard didn't respond. He just sat there as he continued to listen to the thunder roar. He could hear it so well because it was brewing inside of him.

Jonathan the Wise eventually decided to break the awkward silence and said, "Well, goodnight, Leonard the Wise, or whoever you are." He lay his head down as Leonard responded, "Goodnight, Jonathan the Wise."

Leonard didn't lay his head down, but just watched Jonathan the Wise drift off to sleep. He looked around and saw everyone else lying down as the flames of hate continued to burn in his eyes.

Eventually, everyone was fast asleep, and Leonard sat up slowly. He watched Jonathan the Wise as he stood up to make sure he wasn't going to stir. When the coast was clear, he made a beeline to the southeast, which is where the Enclave was from their position. He remembered that from Levi's description of the geography of Bu Zing.

The closer and closer Leonard came to the Enclave as he crossed the Desert of Deception, the louder the thunder got. Eventually, he could see the lightning flashing in the sky just before the thunderclap. He could also see the path to the Enclave. Surprisingly, no Demons tried to attack him. Probably because they were all sleeping in their perches along the path to the Enclave.

Leonard wondered how these creatures could be sleeping through such a tumultuous storm. The rain began to pour down hard, but still, no Demon moved a muscle from their sleeping position. Leonard was rather thankful for that. They just sat in their tree-like perches at the tops of the stone walls that led to the Enclave. They looked a little like gargoyles up there.

As he journeyed on, a chill went up his spine that wasn't from the cold rain. He was surprised how long the night lasted. He might have more time to toy with the Dragon than he originally thought.

As he came close to the Enclave, he saw a giant mountain of stone that looked like a skull. The mouth of the skull was a dark cave and he could see the Dragon's tail sticking out into the light of the storm. Leonard slowly drew his sword as it glided in the sheath and made a scraping sound.

Suddenly, the giant red eyes from the Citadel opened in the mouth of the skull and the Dragon's tail was sucked into the darkness. He heard the deep, booming voice, as well, questioning, "Who dares disturb my slumber?" The eyes rose to a great height and Leonard could tell that meant the Dragon had stood up.

Leonard swallowed hard as he raised his sword to his right side with both hands clenched tightly about it, "I do! Leonard the Wise." By now, all the Demons were awake after hearing the voice of their Ruler.

The Dragon just chuckled sinisterly, "Oh, yes, Leonard." Leonard heard his scale-grinding smile.

Leonard raised his sword a little higher and tried to appear firm, "I'm not afraid of you, beast!"

"You aren't? Then why does your voice tremble?" The Dragon's eyes moved closer to the mouth of the cave as Leonard heard his thunderous footsteps that were almost as loud as the storm's thunder. The lightning flashed and revealed the Dragon's large muzzle that was now sticking out of the cave.

Leonard was slightly scared, but his hate was greater than his fear. He just ignored the Dragon and continued to stand with his sword raised at his side, "I came for my family!"

The Dragon's pupils went thin as he appeared to raise his head and draw his muzzle back into the cave, "Your family? Oh, yes. The Whittens." He smiled once again, as he lowered his head.

Leonard got so angry he began to snarl, "Let them go!"

The Dragon chuckled, again, and then asked, "Or what?"

"I'll slay you."

"Foolish boy. You can't hurt me. I'm beyond your realm." The Dragon walked a little bit further out of the cave and Leonard saw his ginormous, black head when the lightning shot across the sky.

"I don't *think* so!" roared Leonard as he ran and then did a giant leap in the air so that he was eye to eye with the Dragon. Life appeared to move in slow motion as he raised his sword above his head and lightning came down to strike it. When it finally connected, he swung his sword forward and cast the bolt at his target, the Dragon's head.

The bolt struck the Dragon right in the face. It gashed all the way down and across his left eye. Blood began gushing from his wound and pouring down around his now split eye. He roared in pain as Leonard landed in front of him. When the Dragon recovered from the jolt, his eyes glowed with vengeance. Leonard just sheathed his sword and stood fast against him.

"You dare taunt the Dragon?!" roared the Dragon as steam began spewing from his nostrils: steam like from a giant furnace.

He reared back again and then lunged forward with a gaping mouth, blasting fiery fury. The flames seemed to consume Leonard, but when the Dragon's blast was finished, a cloud of smoke could be seen above where he used to be.

Suddenly, the smoke cleared, and you could see Leonard holding his arms across his face in an "X" formation with smoking bracers. He had turned himself into the rain to shield himself from the flames of the Dragon.

The Dragon was now even more furious as he continued to breath smoke from his nostrils. With each breath, came another puff of smoke. Leonard just stood strong and said, "Remember, Dragon, I *can* hurt you."

The Dragon remained silent for a while, but then asked, "Do you proclaim the Prince of Peace as your Ruler?"

Leonard looked up with a determined glare on his face. "Yes, I do."

The Dragon was now completely out of the cave and circling around Leonard. "I will take all that you hold dear and *crucify* it. That includes your Ruler and your *family*!" He shouted the last word and it echoed in Leonard's ears. The boom of his voice was so powerful that it blew Leonard's hair back and caused some of the Demons to fly away in fear.

Leonard had flinched in fear of being barbequed again, but stood back up straight as he realized the Dragon was walking back into his cave. "Why don't you just kill me now?"

The Dragon stopped walking and turned his head around so his shattered eye gleamed in the lightning strike. It was a horrid sight and caused Leonard to wish he hadn't mentioned death. They stared eye to eye for a while and then the Dragon replied, "Because it will be far more enjoyable to torture you and watch you suffer."

Suddenly, Leonard's vision flashed again and he was back in the Greenlands. He was staring across at Jonathan the Wise as the sun began to rise. He didn't remember the trek back and felt rather confused as he looked around at everyone waking up.

Chapter Ten

Battle of the Armies

Today was the day for the battle of the Armies. Leonard didn't know what that exactly meant, but everyone else did. It meant that all six Armies were going to meet on the Planes and fight in epic battle fashion. The Lord's Army would have to descend the Great Ledge before they could enter the battle, but all the other Armies were already down there, ready for combat. Well, except for the Dragon's, of course. They still had to fly there so it wasn't that big of a deal.

Leonard stood up and began dusting himself off as Jonathan the Wise did the same. Leonard finished and then looked around, wondering, "Where are the rest of my friends?"

Suddenly, a group of people in the distance began walking toward them. He couldn't make them out at first, but then he recognized Victor's brawny stature and knew it was the rest of his friends. They all met up around what was left of Jonathan the Wise's and Leonard's fire as they exchanged smiles and embraces. The fire was now just a thin line of smoke reaching toward the sky.

"Ah, did zou hear ze Prince of Peace's teaching, Leonard ze Vise?" asked Victor, just as happy-go-lucky as could be.

Leonard felt a little uneasy about talking about the Prince of Peace's teaching because of how it impacted him and just smiled. "Uh, yeah. I did."

Levi slapped him on the back and smiled, "Well then, you are obviously ready for the battle of the Armies."

Leonard just smiled again as Tang Lo began to see his uneasiness. He became suspicious as he leaned toward Jonathan the Wise and whispered, "What is wrong wit him?"

Jonathan the Wise just smiled and replied, "He's just very young, that's all."

Tang Lo frowned at his answer as he leaned away in confusion. "What?"

Jonathan the Wise just shook his head for Tang Lo to drop the subject and walked toward Leonard to give him a warm embrace. "Leonard the Wise, I am proud of your progress in training and am honored to fight beside you." Jonathan the Wise put his arm around him and Leonard just kind of backed away a little, as if to say, "What are you doing?"

Jonathan the Wise noticed him back away as did everyone. He smiled sheepishly and said, "Leonard the Wise, may I speak with you in private?"

Leonard just frowned as Jonathan the Wise led him a short distance away and then became stern. "Look, young man, I don't know *who* you are, but you've got to fight! It matters not who I think you are. The only opinion that matters in the end is the Trinity's."

Leonard just lowered his head in defeat. "I already tried."

"What do you mean?" questioned Jonathan the Wise as he frowned in confusion and wonder.

Leonard looked up with a sorrowful look on his face. "I tried to kill the Dragon, but for some reason I couldn't."

Jonathan the Wise looked down and began to chuckle. He looked back up and placed his right hand on Leonard's shoulder.

"Son, that's because slaying the Dragon is not your fight. Your fight is in the Lord's Army on the Planes."

"How do you know for sure?"

Jonathan the Wise got close to his face, "Because you are not Jesus Christ." He stepped back and lowered his right hand from Leonard's shoulder. "You are just to be His follower."

Leonard suddenly felt a surge of understanding, again, like when Jesus had finished speaking. They returned to the rest of the group as a trumpet began to blow. Leonard looked up to see who blew it and saw a man standing on a hill with it in his hands. He turned to his companions. "What was that for?"

Tang Lo just looked him straight in the eyes and said, "It is time for battle."

Everyone began congregating in a large company of hundreds and then the trumpet was blown again. The march had begun across the Greenlands to the Great Ledge. Once they descended it, epic battle would consume them.

As they made their journey toward the Great Ledge, the battle of the Armies had already begun on the Planes between the Armies that were already there. At first, Pharaoh's Army dominated the Queen's with his iron chariots, but then the Emperor's Army began to make headway by firing upon his chariots with their cannons. Then, Hitler's Army rolled in with their tanks and just blew everyone to smithereens. It seemed he would dominate, but then the Dragon's Army rained terror down from the sky. This process continued as much blood was shed on the Planes, but the battle had only begun.

The Lord's Army came to the Great Ledge as Jesus stood on the edge. Tang Lo, Leonard, and a bunch of other Arts users stood with Jesus. When he raised his hands, they knew that was the cue to jump. He looked from side to side and then raised his hands in epic fashion. All the Arts users jumped and began to ride the wind on the way down. They all became the wind and seemingly flew.

One of Hitler's tanks saw them coming down the Great Ledge and rolled over to blast away. Leonard saw it and quickly flew toward the Great Ledge and drug his hand against the rocky surface. His eyes glowed and then he placed his hands at his sides like a torpedo. He fell a lot faster than the wind riders, because of his changed weight and better aerodynamics.

The tank was crushed as he smashed down with his feet right on the turret. No one would be making it out of *that* iron pancake.

Tang Lo flew right over Leonard and said, "Good job."

Leonard just smiled and waved as he stood up.

Tang Lo led the rest of the Arts users as the Lord's Army's air support. They flew above the chaos with swords swinging and slashing away. All the rest of the Lord's Army had to descend the Great Ledge by freeclimbing the rock face.

Leonard decided to stand his ground at the bottom of the Great Ledge for his fellow soldiers. He ripped his sword from its sheath and began to put Levi's training to use against the Queen's and the Emperor's men. He was rather swift and effective. As one of the Emperor's men lunged at him, he dodged and made him stab the rock behind him. He followed through by blocking two others' swings and then stabbing him in the back. The two swings he blocked came around again and he quickly took a firm stand on the tank and turned into metal. He used his left arm to block the two swings and then slashed across their guts. They fell on the ground as Leonard began to feel proud of his fighting capabilities. He glanced up to the sky to see how Tang Lo and the Arts users were fairing.

They seemed to have no problem with fighting off the Demons, but then Hitler's air force flew in with guns-a-blazing. Two of the Arts users were gunned down, leaving just twenty-seven in the sky. Thirty of them had jumped, Leonard landed early, and then those two had been shot down. Several Demons took some bullets, too, as they blew away to dust.

Eventually, some of the rest of the Lord's Army made it onto the Planes and began fighting. Tanya Brooks was one of them. Leonard smiled as he watched her roar and slay multiple opponents at once. She was certainly like a phoenix rising from the flame.

The Prince of Peace was on the Planes now, too. The Demons were sure happy to take a swing at Him, as well. One came walking toward Him and said, "I'm going to take your life."

Jesus just calmly replied, "You cannot take what is not yet given." He thrust His right hand toward the Demon, and it sounded like a lion's roar came from it. It blasted the Demon to dust and turned up some soil.

He continued to parade the Planes, offering His services wherever they were needed. It's simple to say that many soldiers heard the Lion's roar.

Hitler's planes began to infuriate Tang Lo as he continued to lose men because of their bullets. He finally just flew toward one of them and grabbed onto the cockpit. He punched through the windshield and proceeded to pull the pilot out. The pilot was soon replaced by him and then he turned Hitler's own guns on him, or at least his Army.

Many of Hitler's planes were shot down by Tang Lo before he was nicked himself. He jumped out and then caught on the wind, again. He placed his arms at his sides and dove back down toward the Planes as the plane he just came from fell in flames. It crashed into a group of enemy soldiers and that pleased him.

Leonard was now being helped in protecting the climbers by Victor and Levi. He rather enjoyed fighting alongside of them but was awfully glad they were on the same side. He lost count of how many men suffered the pain of one of Victor's hatchet throws. Levi was rather deadly and quick with his blade, as well.

They slowly advanced closer to the middle of the Planes, away from the Great Ledge, and seemingly began to win. The Dragon suddenly swooped down and breathed a line of his coursing fire. Many of the Lord's Army were decimated in the flame, including Tanya Brooks. It was a pity that her armor signified her end.

Leonard roared at the Dragon with his rekindled hate. The Dragon just laughed and flew across the Planes, away from him. Leonard viciously hacked and slashed his way across the Planes, trying to follow the Dragon and see where he was going. He created a path through the enemy forces that allowed his companions to advance but didn't really care. He just wanted to get even with the Dragon, again.

"I'll slash his other eye if I have to," thought Leonard as he fought his way across the Planes.

Jonathan the Wise saw him and so did Jesus. Jonathan the Wise turned toward Jesus and he just nodded as if to say, "I'll take care of him."

With that decided, Jonathan the Wise continued to fight as Jesus just followed Leonard through his path of destruction. He wouldn't engage anyone, though. They'd lunge at him and He'd just dodge away, because they weren't allowed to harm Him...yet.

Leonard fought his way across the Planes from the Great Ledge toward the Citadel. He didn't realize that until he saw the Dragon fly up a large hill and enter a castle-like structure at the top. He entered on the left side as Leonard began to struggle to keep up the adrenaline rush.

He was tiring, but then saw one of Pharaoh's chariots rushing him. The horse looked like it was snarling like the Dragon the closer it came to him. At the last minute, he lunged into the back of the chariot with the occupants. He quickly dueled and then helped the rider exit the chariot as the driver continued to charge more soldiers. Leonard then grabbed the driver and threw him out the back. He gripped the reins and snapped them for more speed as he began the ascent up the large, grassy hill toward the Citadel.

There seemed to be no guards when he came to the Citadel, but then he saw them. They clanked in their gray, heavy-grade armor as they approached him with weapons drawn. Their weapons were rifles that looked like stun guns and their armor was also futuristic-looking. Their armor was gray, because they were neutral as to what Ruler they served. They served all the Rulers. At least, that was their coexist oath.

They began shooting at Leonard and he ducked out of their fire, but they got the horse. The horse instantly dropped and caused the chariot to snap off and go flying at the Neutral Guards. It took out one of them, but Leonard still had to deal with the other one. He had hidden himself behind one of the gate's pillars as the stun pellets hit next to him. He quickly grabbed the stone pillar as his eyes glowed and then he charged the Neutral Guard. The Neutral Guard fired many stun pellets right at Leonard, but they just shattered and sparked on his stone-like body with no effect to him. The Neutral Guard was eventually flattened by his bull rush, but more of them showed up. Leonard just puffed and then readied his blade for more action.

Meanwhile, inside the Citadel's throne room, they heard a thunderous boom and were all surprised. They suddenly realized that that meant the Dragon had returned from the battle of the Armies. His boiling, red eyes were eventually seen in the darkness of the tunnel and they could also hear his violent breaths. He stepped into the light of the room with his face showing and Queen Victoria cattily said, "Back so soon?"

The Dragon just snarled as saliva dripped from his jaw. He sucked it in and then proceeded to walk further into the throne room. You could tell how tired his steps were from how hard they jolted against the floor. The battle appeared to have wearied him. He went to speak, but then they heard a commotion outside the throne room doors. They all looked toward the two Neutral Guards that were on the inside and they shrugged. The Dragon began to walk toward the doors as the Neutral Guards went to open them.

Suddenly, they flew open, smashing the Neutral Guards against the wall and revealing a rather intimidating scene. Leonard stood, hunched over with an unconscious Neutral Guard hanging from each of his hands. His arms were flexing under the weight of their armor, but then he dropped them. They clanked to the floor as he stood up straight and began to walk into the throne room with a swagger.

Napoleon Bonaparte jumped up from his seat and shouted, "How *dare* you enter ze trone room by force?!"

The Dragon's pupils went thin as he stared at Leonard. Everyone else shared Napoleon's disgust, except Queen Victoria. She looked at Leonard with a look of curiosity as she blankly asked, "Yes? Who are you and what is your business here, young man?"

Leonard just slowly drew his sword as he continued to walk toward the Dragon, who was now in the middle of the room, almost filling it, "I've come for the Dragon's head."

The Dragon just smiled as he noticed something Leonard didn't. There was a Neutral Guard sneaking up behind him with his rifle ready. Leonard raised his sword, but then got shot in the back and fell to the floor. A painful sting rang throughout his body as he lay on the floor, twitching from the stun pellet.

Chapter Eleven

The Penalty

The Neutral Guard walked over to the downed Leonard and asked the Rulers, "What do you wish done with him?"

The Dragon turned to the rest of the Rulers and said, "Clearly, he should be punished."

They all nodded rather quickly in agreement, except Queen Victoria. She was still curious as to who he was. She held up her hand, "Wait. Who is this seemingly brave and rash young man?"

The Dragon turned back to Leonard and hung his head over him with a smile. He looked down and said, "Leonard the Wise."

Napoleon turned to Queen Victoria with his hands clenching the arms of his throne. "He is one of ze Wise?! How can zis be?!"

Hitler just puffed, "Huh! He is neizer Vise nor bold, but razher foolish."

Ramses decided to chime in. "He should still be punished, no matter *who* he is."

"Oui. What shall be his penalty?" asked Napoleon as he jerked his head and then turned to the Dragon.

The Dragon just smiled, once again, as he let his saliva drip on Leonard's body. "Death."

Suddenly, someone was standing in the doorway to the throne room and calmly said, "He will not be punished."

The Dragon quickly looked up and began to glare when he saw who it was. It was the Prince of Peace, the One Ruler Who had never stepped a foot in the Citadel, but now contradicted the majority vote.

Leonard had come around and been taken aside by the Neutral Guard that stunned him. He stood with his arms pinned behind him as Jesus stepped forward into the throne room. He still couldn't see His face but was still rather glad to see the rest of Him.

The Dragon practically growled as he asked, "And why *not*?"

"Yes, do you propose he is not guilty?" added Ramses with a point of his finger in Leonard's direction.

Jesus continued to walk toward the other Rulers as he glanced toward Leonard. "Oh no, he *is* guilty."

"Then what do you mean coming in here and demanding he not be punished? Does he not deserve to be punished?" questioned Queen Victoria as she frowned at Jesus' unique court manners.

Jesus just laughed as He stood before the Dragon and felt his hot breaths, "He is worthy of his punishment, but what if someone else was to take it for him?"

"Who do zou propose vould be villing do such a thing?" asked Hitler as the Dragon just began to smile, because he knew where Jesus was going with His argument. He was going to rather enjoy this.

"I am."

Everyone was in shock, but of course, not the Dragon. He just leaned down close to Jesus' face and breathed on Him, saying, "Gladly."

Suddenly, the Dragon raised his foot of sharp claws and came crashing down on Jesus. The blow knocked Him to the floor and tore his white robe from his body. Another slash cut his entire side open and cast His blood on the wall next to where Leonard was being restrained. Every blow seemed to echo as Leonard cried out for His Ruler.

The Dragon just smiled with a sinister gleam in his eye. He would swing even harder with every slash as blood spilled on the stone floor and Jesus' body flopped about with little resistance.

Suddenly, Leonard's vision flashed with the sound of thunder and then he was kneeling back at the Enclave, where a thunderstorm was obviously brewing again. As he looked up, he saw Jesus hanging on a cross stripped of his garments, but you could barely make out his bodily form. There wasn't a place on His body that was not torn open and gushing blood. It dripped at the foot of the cross he hung on as Leonard cried and tried to move closer to where Jesus' cross sat atop the skull-shaped, rock structure. "No, no, no." He just kept repeating that word as the lightning shot across the sky behind Jesus and he realized he could see His face now. He focused more and then reared back in shock of who it was. It was *his*. Not his face from Bu Zing, but his face in the real world. Lightning shot across the sky and Jesus' body went limp as he simply said with his last breath, "It is finished."

Leonard returned to crying out and reaching toward Him, but then he felt a hand on his shoulder and his vision flashed again. He was now standing on the Beach of Beauty, looking at a hole that had been made in the Bedrock. It appeared to be a tomb with a giant stone rolled to the side of the entrance.

Leonard was still crying when he heard Jonathan the Wise's voice come from behind him. He turned around and the first words from his mouth were, "Why'd He have to die?!"

Jonathan the Wise looked down at the trembling Leonard with a look of compassion as he answered his loaded question, "Because the penalty had to be paid." He placed his hand on his shoulder.

"What penalty?" asked Leonard as he stayed in his kneeling position.

"Sin, which results in the penalty of death. 'For the wages of sin is death, but the gift of God is eternal lifelife,'" explained Jonathan the Wise as he took away his hand from Leonard's shoulder.

Leonard sat there in thought for a while as he tried to sniff his tears away. They slowly stopped falling. Then he looked back up at Jonathan the Wise in wonder. "How do I receive this gift?"

Jonathan the Wise smiled. "By merely believing and having Faith that He took the penalty for you. Believe on the Lord Jesus Christ and you shall be saved, Leonard the Wise." He pointed toward the empty tomb and Leonard remembered all the Sunday school lessons about the Gospel.

Tears began to trickle down Leonard's face as he simply stated, "I do. I do believe on the Lord Jesus Christ."

Suddenly, his vision flashed again, and he was staring at his ceiling, crying. He quickly stopped crying and sat up in bed to look around. He saw that it was for sure his room with the TV on his wooden dresser just across from him and his nightstand just to his right. His fingers fumbled with the switch to his lamp on the nightstand as he tried to let his eyes adjust.

Eventually, Leonard's bedroom was dimly lit by his lamplight and he felt the need to get on his knees on the floor. The soft carpet was rather comforting to him as a sign of home as he clasped his hands together and began to whisper, "Lord, I thank You for showing me what to do. I don't know if what happened in Bu Zing counts, so I just wanted to say, I believe in You, Jesus. You are my Lord and Savior. Thank You!" There was a brief pause and then he finished with, "I'm all Yours! Amen."

When he looked back up, he saw his clock under his lamp on the nightstand. It said that it was 2:34 in the morning. Seeing the time made him yawn and then crawl back into bed. It took a little while for him to fall back asleep with all the excitement that rang through his body. He had just given his life to God!

Eventually, his eyelids fell shut and he breathed softly and slept soundly.

Chapter Twelve
The Miracle of Music

The next time Leonard's eyes opened was because of the bright sunlight shining through his blinds and into his eyes. It was a beautiful morning and he couldn't wait to get up!

As he dressed himself, he suddenly remembered what a mess his family was in and some of his joy fluttered away. It was replaced with sadness as he realized no one would probably care that he was a Christian now, except maybe Tanya Brooks, of course. He smiled at the thought of having seen how Tanya might look in the future and then finished pulling his shirt on.

Once his shirt was over his head, he spied his radio in a corner of his room, collecting dust. It had been a while since he used it because he had a Smartphone and all. He picked it up and dusted it off with his hand. It was very gently placed on his nightstand beside his clock as he knelt in front of it. He turned it on and was surprisingly happy to turn it to 96.9 F.M., which was Air1.

The voices of the morning show people could barely be heard, so he turned up the volume. He heard them announce, "And next up we have a great song by Kutless called, 'What Faith Can Do.'"

He heard intro music and then the lead singer's voice singing,

What Faith Can Do

"Everybody falls sometimes
You gotta find the strength to rise
Up from the ashes
And make a new beginning."

Suddenly, the words and the rhythm just hit him in the right place, and he began to cry, because he was amazed how awesome God is. The song continued as he just sat there and listened, eyes filled with tears of joy. When it came to the beginning of the chorus, the words seemed meant just for him as they were,

"I've seen
Dreams that move the mountains…"

The chorus ended with the simple truth,

"That's what Faith can do."
- Kutless

Having been energized by the chorus, Leonard wiped his face and stood up to finish getting dressed as the song continued to play in the background.

The song faded as he prepared to go downstairs for breakfast. He turned off the radio when it went back to the morning show hosts and ventured downstairs. There was no one else up. It was just him moving about the kitchen, preparing his bowl of Captain Crunch Berries. The sound of the cereal was rather loud as it hit the Corelle bowl. At least it seemed loud because there was no other noise to be heard. Then came the crunching in his mouth.

It seemed very odd to be alone at such a young age as he peered around the kitchen.

He looked through the doorway to the dining room and saw the pool through the French doors. It reminded him of a couple days ago and he had to shake his head at how much had changed in just a night. His whole *life* had changed, and no one knew it, except God, of course. It's amazing how such a great amount of change can be so quiet sometimes. Well, it seemed to be quiet to Leonard, but God was working behind the scenes. Leonard just didn't see it yet.

While Leonard ate his breakfast, Jessica woke up at the foot of her bed. She had fallen asleep with half of her body on the bed and half on the floor. Her back ached as she tried to sit up straight. She pressed against her lower back to try and bend and stretch it. Her hands then moved to her hair that was in a rather tangled mess. She scratched her head a little as she yawned and then saw the empty bed.

Suddenly, the memory of yesterday's quarrel with David came rushing back to her and tears began to fill her eyes. Once again, she felt the need to ask, "Why?"

She fought her way to her feet and then used the bed to get to her nightstand on the left side. She was going to turn on some music to try and help her prepare for the day. The first thing was, of course, waking up all the way. Then came freshening up to try and enhance the beautiful woman she already was. Messy hair and all.

Her fingers fumbled over the screen to her Smartphone as she scrolled her playlists, trying to decide what she was in the mood for. Nothing seemed to spark the right feeling of inspiration, but then she got an idea.

"Air1 always seems to have inspiring music on. I'll just go to Air1.com," thought Jessica as she pulled up her web browser and typed it in. The website finished loading and the purple button reading "Listen Now" was clearly visible. She tapped on it and was instantly taken aback by the song she heard.

The smoky, alto voice of Lauren Daigle came over Jessica's phone singing,

You Say

*"I keep fighting voices in mind that say I'm not enough
Every single lie that tells me I will never measure up."*

Jessica couldn't hold it in and burst into tears as she cupped her hands over her mouth. She continued to listen to the song, crying harder with every lyric.

*"Am I more than just the sum of every high and every low?
Remind me once again just who I am, because I need to know
You say I am loved..."*
- Lauren Daigle

The song went on as Jessica dwelt on the single thought that she was loved, until the simple last phrase of the chorus hit her right in the heart and sent her to the floor. She couldn't believe how the words seemed just meant for her. She looked up with tears pouring down her face and said, "Thank you, God. I am Yours," her head fell back down, "and I believe what you say of me."

The song finished up as she climbed up and moved toward the master bathroom to freshen up. She took her phone with her, hungering for more inspirational music from God using Air1.

Meanwhile, clear in Dayton, Ohio, David was waking up from a not so comfortable position, too. He had fallen asleep in his car last night, after barely resisting the temptation to drink again. He rubbed his eyes as he tried to fix them on his surroundings. His car was still in the bar's parking lot. He looked down toward the cup holders where his keys were and saw his wife's sunglasses. A smile came over his face as he remembered their honeymoon in Hawaii.

"She was so beautiful," thought David as he picked up the sunglasses and began to admire them. A Voice inside of him told him, "She still is. You just haven't taken the time to notice."

He sorrowfully placed the sunglasses back in the cup holder of his car and grabbed his keys. The engine started and he found himself feeling the strange urge to turn on the radio. He pushed the power button to the radio and it just happened to be on 88.3 F.M., which is Air1 as well. It was the beginning to the Sanctus Real song, "Lead Me,"

Lead Me

"I look around
And see my wonderful life
Almost perfect
From the outside."

David instantly found himself interested as he just sat in his car and continued to listen to the song.

"In picture frames
I see my beautiful wife..."
- Sanctus Real

David couldn't hold it in anymore. He had been trying to fight back tears like the "strong man" he was, but after the mention of his beautiful wife, his heart melted. Tears trickled down his face as the song continued to move him with every word. The one phrase that kept echoing in his mind was, "Lead me."

David turned the keys in his car so that the engine wasn't running anymore, but the song was still playing. He felt the need to get on his knees, but he couldn't do that in the car. He found himself opening the driver's door, just so he could step out onto the pavement and kneel. It wasn't comfortable, but it *was* peaceful. The song continued in the background as he prayed with his hands lifted up. "God, I haven't shown my wife the love I should have. I haven't taught my children the way I should have." His lips quivered as he continued to pray, "I haven't served *You* in the way I should have, but I can't do this alone, God. I need you to lead me, so I can lead them. I'm *not* strong enough," he dropped his raised hands to his sides and then raised his right fist, "but You *are*. Lord God *help* me. I'm Yours."

He lowered his fist, once again, as the song slowly faded, and he looked back up toward Heaven. He instantly felt empowered as he wiped the tears from his face and said, "Thank you."

He couldn't get in his car fast enough to start it again and begin the drive home, but then he remembered Cyndi Dunne. He didn't want to be tempted again, so he made a difficult decision as he pulled out his phone. It might have been the least professional way to fire someone, via a phone call, but he *really* didn't want to be tempted by her again.

The phone began to ring as he held it up to his ear. Cyndi was rather enthused when she saw that it was her boss calling her and couldn't push the green answer button fast enough.

"Hello, David," came Cyndi's seducing voice over the phone.

David swallowed hard, but then did what he had to do. "Hello, Miss Dunne. I am calling about your performance the other night. I believe it was very unprofessional and I cannot tolerate it in my workplace, so I'm afraid I will have to let you go."

That wasn't exactly what Cyndi was hoping for and she didn't even respond before she hung up. David just sighed in relief that that was over and then put his car in drive.

The trip home didn't seem to take too long because he found himself trying to plan out what his wife would say in the conversation they were about to have. He finally caught himself and said, "No. You need to stop assuming what she's going to say. You might have known her for a long time, but you've still got a lot to learn."

He smiled at his own conviction, but thanked God for it instead of being proud.

A little while later, Jessica heard a car pull into the driveway and rushed to her bathroom window with great hope. She cupped her hand over her mouth and began to cry when she saw that it was her husband stepping out of the car. He felt the need to look up toward their bathroom window and saw his wife in tears. He began to cry, too, as he smiled, waved, and then ran for the front door.

When he made it through the front door and to the foot of the steps, he found his beautiful wife standing at the top with brushed hair and all. It was a rather romantic scene, depicting the climb he must make to lead his family. He slowly walked up the stairs as Jessica cried more and more with every step. He couldn't help but apologize with every step, too, "I'm sorry…I haven't loved you in the way I should. I'm sorry…I haven't paid attention. I'm sorry that I have assumed you to be someone you're not. I'm sorry…I haven't taken the time to learn more about you." He began to cry deeply, "And I'm sorry that I have not helped you raise our children like I promised on our wedding day."

By this time, he had made it to the top and Jessica just stood there in front of him with hands cupped on her face.

"I'm sorry, too," was all Jessica had to say as she opened her arms to her husband and he gladly embraced her.

Suddenly, a thought dawned on Jessica and she surprisingly asked without hesitation, "But what about Cyndi Dunne?"

David could have gotten angry with his wife, but he just smiled and said, "Honey, I let her go this morning."

Jessica gasped at her husband's act of integrity and then he continued with his smile, "So, Mrs. Whitten, we currently have a job opening at my company. I guess what I mean to say is, Mrs. Whitten, will you be my secretary?"

Jessica began to smile, too, at her husband's playfulness and couldn't help but plant a big old kiss on his lips.

Leonard smiled as he watched from below. He was so happy how God had changed his world around. Well, everyone had heard their special music, except Dana and Matt, but their time would come, eventually...

Words of Wisdom

The Imagination Gift: Dream One: The Kingdom of Chaos was originally created in the dining room of the *Dairy Store* at *Young's Jersey Dairy*, which is why I wanted to dedicate this story to them. I was in bussing when the idea came to me. It just kind of escalated from there to being a four-part book series.

In this story, I wanted to show the Truth, as I try to do in all my stories. When we work with someone, we tend to forget that they have lives outside of work that might be a completely different atmosphere than we think. The moral of this story is that there's a lot more going on that we can't see, which is a lesson I've come to greatly enjoy. It has a sense of Faith, because Hebrews 11:1 says, "Faith is the substance of things hoped for, the evidence of things not seen."

2 Corinthians 5:7 also says, "For we walk by faith, not by sight."

There's a lot more to that phrase than meets the eye, and that's really what I wanted to show in this dramatic story.

Having it placed in Springfield, Ohio, made it a lot easier to identify with the story and that's another thing I wanted it to be. I wanted it to be a story where no matter who you are, there's something you can relate to. That's the way Jesus taught through His parables and that's what inspired me to write.

As for the subtitle, it is called, "The Kingdom of Chaos" for both the real-world experience and the dream world experience.

The Kingdom of Chaos is the dream world, Bu Zing, while it is also the real-world Leonard lives in. His family appears to have everything (the kingdom) but is truly falling apart at the seams (of chaos). It is basically a story of vanity turned into victory.

Now, there's probably a decent amount of questionable material in this story that I should address. The top one is probably the immodesty aspect. In Ephesians 5:11-13, we are instructed to make manifest the darkness through reproof. That is the foundation of why I have it in this story. I want people to understand that it *does* exist, and we need to confront it and stop trying to hide it in the back corner. You can't hide the Truth. And the Truth is that there is light *and* darkness on this earth, because it is sin cursed. There will always be light and darkness on this earth, until it is destroyed in order to make a new one, where there will be *no* darkness at all.

Please, don't think that I am promoting the idea of immodesty by having it in here. I hope you can clearly see my reproving of it. It is important to me to reprove it and teach others against it, because I was addicted to pornography before I became a true believer. That's another way this story is from the heart.

I also mentioned homosexuality and transgenderism with Levi's joke as a little way of stating reproof toward them.

You are probably also wondering why I lashed out at psychology. That is because of Ephesians 5:11-13, again, but also because I have seen Christians becoming more apt to quote the words of an atheist rather than the Word of God. They even tend to *follow* the words of an atheist sometimes over the Word of God.

Psychology was founded by a devout atheist named Sigmund Freud, who said he wanted to prove that man does not need God. Some might say he has succeeded when you look around today.

There is no way psychology and Christianity can mix. There is no such thing as "Christian psychology." You can build up a building and make it look just as pretty as you want, but in the end, if the foundation is still weak and corrupt, the building is still going to fall. Call to mind the parable of the man who built his house on the sand and the man who built his house on the Rock. The sand is psychology and the Rock is of course the Word of God or God, Himself.

There is deeper discussion I could go into, but I don't want to spend all my words talking about psychology.

Another aspect you might question is perhaps the "promotion" of Eastern mysticism in the dream world of Bu Zing. The whole idea of this four-part book series is to show the progression of Leonard using his imagination gift for God. So, in the first book, his imagination will still be caught up in worldly things. Since dreams are founded a lot on our imagination, it would make sense for his first dream to still include some wrong things. Especially since he wasn't even a Christian yet. I hope that makes sense.

In talking about dreams, I hope I was clear in the way I said it at the beginning that God did not *give* Leonard the dream, but rather, *used* the dream to show him what he needed to do. That might sound a little confusing, but it makes sense when you rightly divide the Scriptures as 2 Timothy 2:15 recommends. Dreams and visions have passed away in this dispensation of Grace.

I also want to address the crucifixion scene at the Enclave when he sees Jesus' face as his own. I am *not* promoting the idea that we can somehow save ourselves. It is meant to symbolize how Jesus took our penalty and basically became us, in the sense that He took our place.

Ephesians 2:8-9 says, "For by grace are ye saved through faith; and that not of yourselves: it is the gift of God: Not of works, lest any man should boast."

I pray you enjoyed reading *The Imagination Gift: Dream One: The Kingdom of Chaos* and were able to learn some important lessons from it. The next one in the series will be called, "The

Imagination Gift: Dream Two: The Ring of Purity." It will take place as he is going through puberty at twelve-years-old.

If you have any more thoughts on *The Imagination Gift: Dream One: The Kingdom of Chaos* that I didn't cover, please email me at micahk.rom.12.1@att.net or call or text me at (937) 244-1181. May grace be with you!